# POST-APOCALYPTIC
# NOMADIC WARRIORS

**A Duck & Cover Adventure Book 1**

Benjamin Wallace

ISBN-13: 978-1478224983
ISBN-10: 1478224983

Cover design by Monkey Paw Creative.

*For my wife and kids.*
*Thanks for understanding.*

From the pages of the best-selling Duck & Cover Adventures comes thirteen stories of those who survived the apocalypse. Some would go on to be heroes, others villains, some were dogs and will stay dogs, but they all must contend with the horrors of the new world and find a way to survive in the wasteland that was America.

**Get this laugh-out-loud collection of stories from the Duck & Cover Adventures post-apocalyptic series now when you sign up for my Readers' Group.**

To get your copy of TALES OF THE APOCALYPSE and be the first to know about new releases and other exclusive content, you just need to tell me where to send it.

Visit
**http://benjaminwallacebooks.com/join-my-readers-group/**
to get your free book now.

# Prelude

---

*Even a mushroom cloud has a silver lining.*

*No one ever sees the good in an apocalypse. And that's understandable. A lot of bad things happen when the world blows up. But then it's all crying about the loss of family and the failure of our society. "Waaah, waaah, waaah, what have we done?"*

*Sure, there's that. But what about the good things brought about by the end of the world? Global warming? It's no longer a problem. And with no more global warming, there are no more whiny hippies.*

*True, it's not all green trees and dead hippies. There are real dangers out there: toxins, disease, big scary bears that have mutated to become bigger and scarier.*

*But here—here in the walls of your city—lies hope. Look around. You've already overcome so much. You've beaten the elements. You've provided food for an entire community. You've managed to live together without killing one another or being annoyed by the stink that most of you are putting off.*

*And, there in that willingness to turn your nose, not up in the air, but toward your funky smelling brethren, lies hope. Hope that we can rebuild this world. Into a braver world, a saner world—a braver world that's much more sane.*

*A world where no child need cry for dinner. A world where no child need cry because he is afraid. A world where no child need cry because you didn't buy him that ring pop at checkout, even though you know that he'll never finish it and it will just end up a sticky mass of carpet lint and hair somewhere under the seat of the car. A world where no child need cry for want of shelter or love. A world where that child will finally just shut his cake hole.*

*This is your chance to make the world the way you want it to be. A loving world. A free world.*

*Are you going to surrender this chance? God, or Russia, or somebody, has seen fit to wipe the slate clean. Now we can apply what we know not to do to make a better world for our children—and their children, and their children, and maybe a few generations beyond that.*

*You've already assumed the right to govern yourself, the responsibility to function under a social contract that apparently didn't mandate bathing.*

*You are now free men and women. Are you going to let these men that gather at your gates take that from you? Just because they're stronger? Just because they have an army of merciless killers? Just because they armed that army with chains and blades? And harnessed the power of the mighty and noble buffalo and turned them against you as the menacing war bison? Are you? Or do you accept this responsibility, this glorious burden, to wrestle from these ashes of mankind a better kind of man?*

*Stand. Stand against this threat. Stand with your heads held high—for you are the true possessors of this world's future. Stand proud. And I will stand with you.*

*This is our world to rebuild. Not theirs. Ours. So let's not fuck it up.*

*- The post-apocalyptic nomadic warrior, from a speech given at the gates of Eternal Hope, Colorado, moments before the Massacre of Eternal Hope, Colorado.*

1
———

Jimmy Edwards had touched his first breast in the big steel barn that stood in the middle of the North Texas prairie. It was a girl's breast; it had belonged to Susan Gilmore, and the contact had been purely accidental.

The two had been playing tag at a birthday party. Jimmy was It and Susan ducked into the barn with the boy close behind her. Giggling as she ran, she tried to decide if she was going to let the boy catch her. She thought he was cute, so her plan was to pretend to let the boy corner her and maybe, just maybe, let him tag her a couple of times here and there.

Her plan had not accounted for the wasp. As she rounded the corner into the barn, it buzzed so close to her face that she would swear she could feel the air from its wings on her nose.

Squealing, she turned to run away from the yellow-and-black threat.

Jimmy, his arms outstretched, was not prepared for her sudden turn. His young hand filled with boob. A brief moment of realization overcame him and he smiled just before his head collided with Susan Gilmore's face, bloodied her nose, and knocked her to the cement floor of the big steel barn.

Apologies spewed from his lips as he tried to help her up, but Susan Gilmore had decided that she didn't like Jimmy anymore and she slapped away his hand. Gripping her nose and tilting her head back, she ran off to find her mom.

Jimmy stared at his hand in amazement. He vowed never to wash it again.

Through sputtering gasps, Susan told her mother about the wasp and the collision that had bloodied her nose, probably ruined her looks, and threatened her future social life.

Jimmy found his friends and told them about the boob.

For many years the boob touching and nose breaking were the most noteworthy thing to ever happen in the big steel barn. Then the world blew up.

After the apocalypse, the barn transitioned from a mythical location that had grown infamous through playground lore into the administration building of the town of New Hope.

Weddings, baptisms, elections, chili contests, and more soon trumped the tag incident as the most important events to occur in the building.

A democracy had been formed in its now-sacred walls; a constitution was written and ratified. This social contract between three dozen citizens had been put into print, signed, framed, and hung on the wall conveniently covering a verse of Sharpie scrawled graffiti that read, "Jim was it, grabbed a tit, Susan threw a big fit."

From that day on, all town business was conducted in the big steel barn.


"Vocation?"

"Post-apocalyptic nomadic warrior."

"Nomad," the man said to himself as he scratched at a piece of paper with the nub of a pencil.

"I'm sorry. I didn't say nomad. Post-apocalyptic nomadic warrior."

"What's the difference?"

"It's a pretty big difference."

Roy Tinner was a balding man and refused to admit it. He sat on the town council and had volunteered long ago to interview any visitors that may wander into the gates of his fair town. Though small in stature, and more than a little heavyset, he viewed himself as the first and best line of defense the town of New Hope had against the threat of immigrants, idiots, and those who happened to be both.

"Fine, I'll put nomadic warrior."

"But, that's not it. It's post-apocalyptic nomadic warrior."

Roy looked up from the handwritten form. "Look. You can't have a time reference in your vocation."

"Yes, I can."

"Who does that? No one does that. Farmers don't call themselves pre-winter harvesters. There's no point. A farmer is a farmer whenever he's a farmer. Same with a nomadic warrior or … whatever."

"I'm not a farmer, good sir. I could have been a farmer. I could have been anything: a water purifier, gasoline refiner, scavenger, hunter, gatherer, post-apocalyptic dentist …

"But I chose to be a post-apocalyptic nomadic warrior. And, in doing so, I have mastered the skills necessary to survive the mutants, toxins, gangs, and other dangers in the wasteland. I can survive in the Great Western Wastes, the Poisoned Pacific Northwest, or Detroit.

"I have studied weaponology, mechanics, electronics, and engineering. I can weld and shoot straighter than most any man.

"I have studied psychology, strategy, and Dale Carnegie.

"It's for all of these reasons and more that I ask you to, please, list my occupation as post-apocalyptic nomadic warrior."

The apocalypse had bred a tremendous amount of weirdos and Roy Tinner had met his fair share. Many had genuinely gone crazy dealing with the devastation and loss of family and friends. Others had seen the world-ending event as a chance to start over, redefined themselves, and created a life they could never have achieved in a civilized society.

Some claimed to be celebrities; if they didn't resemble the famous person, they would claim that they had been disfigured by one of the many agents used in the warheads.

A few claimed to be royalty, declaring themselves kings or queens of vast swaths of land or states, if not the country or continent.

The man who sat before him, however, was not trying to make such a claim. This nomad that sat before the councilman believed every word he had said. Etching on his duster was proof of countless days spent in the wasteland—the canvas was frayed by nights spent on rock and rough ground. Calloused hands told of a life of physical labor. A sharpness in the nomad's eyes convinced the councilman that the man in front of him was not crazy.

Conviction, not pride, had prompted the man before him to request the title. The councilman could see that. Like the master mason or the decorated soldier, it was respect that this man was looking for. Respect, not for himself, but for the craft he studied. An acknowledgment of the dedication, the thousands of hours spent mastering the skills that defined his ilk was all he sought. The recognition was not only for himself, but also for others in his trade.

Raising a soiled handkerchief from the desk, the councilman dabbed at the sweat on his brow as he studied the man. Roy could respect the nomad for making a fuss over the entry on the form—but he didn't have to.

Roy picked up the pencil and began to write, "Nomadic Warrior."

"You can't spell apocalyptic, can you?"

"Of course I can spell apocalyptic! We've all been living in a post-apocalyptic world for seven years now. You don't think I've had to write apocalyptic over and over again?" He looked back to the paper and paused.

"A-p-o-c-a-l-y-p-t-i-c."

The councilman took a deep breath and scribbled furiously, "... alyptic nomadic ..." he trailed off and finished writing the full occupation, curving the last few letters of "warrior" up the edge of the page to fit.

"Name?"

"That's up to you."

"I beg your pardon?"

"Well, not you per say. The town."

"What are you talking about?"

"The first rule of being a post-apocalyptic nomadic warrior is that you don't have a name. Eventually, the people I help will give me a nickname, never wanting to know the real me."

"What?"

"That's okay. It makes writing the folklore easier."

"That's ridiculous."

"No, it's not. All post-apocalyptic nomadic warriors don't have names."

"Sure they do."

"No, they don't. Did the man with no name have a name? No, he didn't. What's-his-face didn't have one either. Neither did the stranger."

Before the apocalypse, Roy Tinner's blood pressure had been high, a condition the doctors had attributed to overeating and overreacting to just about everything. Even though the doctors vaporized, melted, exploded, rotted, or had been eaten, like most of the world's population, he felt it was best to behave as though his stress levels had not been reduced since the sweeping destruction of society and man.

Relaxing had never come easy to him, but he did his best to ease the muscles in his neck and smiled at the infuriating nomad. "Well, what should I write down?"

"Just leave it blank. You can fill it in later once I'm given a nickname."

"I'm thinking of one right now," the councilman muttered as he struck a line through the field on the form. "And why do you want to become a citizen of the town of New Hope?"

"Oh. I don't want to be a citizen."

"Then what are you doing here?"

"The way it usually works is that I help out a bit—fix crops or irrigation systems, help out rebuilding things, that kind of stuff. Then, someone will get sick or hurt. I'll come through, against impossible odds, endear myself to the town, get the girl, and be on my way."

An image of the nomad hitting the ground, face first, outside the gates of the town flickered in his mind and generated a genuine smile across Roy Tinner's face. Seeing it happen would be easy enough, but the mayor wanted the nomad here.

Frustration drove the huff from Roy's plump lips; he grabbed the form from the desk and tore it up.

"Is there a problem?" the nomad asked.

Tinner grunted as he pushed himself away from the desk. The squeaky protest of a broken caster rang out as the chair rolled back a few feet and ground to a sudden halt. Inertia tried to topple the heavyset man from his seat when the office chair came to a jarring stop. Weight won out against physics; the councilman fell to his feet and stood to cross the room.

"That form was for new citizens. I'm going to need a different one."

His destination was a beaten filing cabinet, but he made sure to cross in front of two mayoral election posters on the near wall. These two campaign ads represented the fledgling democracy that was New Hope, but they looked as if they belonged in a high school hallway, not a functioning post-apocalyptic society.

Incumbent Mayor Wilson sought a seventh term and promised to "Give Everyone Hope." An illustration of the smiling public official lacked just a little in proportion, but was a fair depiction of the man the nomad had met at the town gates. The candidate's arms were opened wide. A welcoming smile beamed across his lips.

Roy Tinner stopped in front of the Wilson campaign poster and blocked it from the nomad's line of sight, leaving only the "Tinner for Mayor" poster visible.

"Keep Hope Alive," was the line that underscored the poorly rendered stick figure that the nomad could only assume was supposed to be councilman Roy with his arms crossed. Heavy lines above the eyes indicated a sterner approach to governing, or hairy eyebrows.

Roy reached the filing cabinet, wrestled the top drawer open, and thumbed through a series of handwritten forms. Creaks groaned from the cabinet as it strained to support the large frame that leaned on it for support. Heavy breaths emanated from the councilman as he concentrated.

"How's the campaign going?" The nomad now saw the furled brow, depicted with multiple marker lines in the poster, reflected on the man himself.

Tinner grunted and continued to leaf through the pages.

"When's the election?"

Roy glanced over the top of the papers. "That's town business," he said and licked his thumb again to continue the search for the document.

The nomad nodded and decided to give up the pursuit of small talk. But when Roy moved on to another drawer, he felt the urge to fill the silence.

"Your town sure has a lot of paperwork."

Roy grunted again. This time it was in pleasant agreement. He had designed every form in the filing cabinet. One final stroke of his thumb against his tongue helped him through five more pages.

"Ah, here it is." Roy sat back in the chair. Four thrusts of his hips brought him back to the table where he slapped down the blank piece of paper. "The form for transient assholes."

"Hey now. I'm just here to help."

"And how can you help?"

"My skills are useful in many areas. Do you need any rare antibiotics retrieved from a hostile area?"

"No, we've got plenty of medicine: penicillin, painkillers, varying strengths of Advil." Roy counted the medicines off on plump fingers.

"Are your crops dying and you don't know why?"

"Bumper crops."

"Anyone disappear mysteriously while strolling outside of the city walls?"

Roy shook his head, "All strollers accounted for."

"How about—"

"Look. We don't need your help. We're doing just fine here. We don't need pharmacists or farmers. We've got plenty of welders and ranchers. I don't think there is anything you could do ... unless."

For the first time since greeting the nomad, his brow unfurled. Roy spotted an opportunity. Despite his more annoying qualities, the nomad appeared to be in excellent shape. He was fit, and not just for a wanderer of the wasteland.

The Tinner Titans kickball team was playing in the championship against the only other team in town and had need of a shortstop; Mrs. Ellison had been placed on the injured list since an unfortunate cakewalk accident earlier in the week.

As coach, Tinner would win bragging rights over the mayor if his team could beat Wilson's Wild Ones. This nomad before him could be the ringer he needed.

Roy leaned forward in his chair, "As a post-apocalyptic nomadic warrior, you must have excellent hand-eye coordination."

Mirroring the lean, the nomad nodded his response.

"You roam the lands—your thighs must be tremendous."

The nomad leaned back, shifted in his seat, and nodded with less enthusiasm.

Roy leaned back in the chair. The caster chirped. Roy smiled, displaying an orthodontist's dream. He sprung the question, "Do you play kickball, Mr. No Name?"

"Not since elementary school. No."

Roy tapped the eraser against the metal desk and dropped the pencil. "Well, then, I think we're done here. It seems we have little need for a non-kickball playing post-apocalyptic nomadic warrior here in New Hope."

"Maybe not now. But as soon as you ask me to leave, trouble will show up at your door."

"Trouble? What trouble? I don't know if you've noticed this in all of your nomadic wandering or not, but the post-apocalyptic world isn't all that bad.

"In fact, we the people of New Hope kind of like it. Things are quiet. We're all neighbors again. There is no TV to distract us, no rat race to frustrate us, and the weather has been fairly pleasant."

"Complacency precedes catastrophe, or so they say," the nomad said.

"Who say?"

"I say."

"You say?"

"I say."

"Well, let me say this—we are hardly complacent. We have planted our fields to provide enough food to last through winter, medical stores to cover any ailment, and doctors to tell us what that ailment is.

"We have shelter, a well and filtration system for endless drinking water. We're raising livestock. We've formed a government. We are hardly complacent. We are prepared."

"That's why you're in danger."

Roy Tinner had been called many names in his life: fat, bastard, and fat bastard among other things. Some of these things dealt with hygiene issues, others with his taste in clothes, music, and athletic proficiency. Once, he was called an ass in one language while someone else called him a hole in a completely different language. Of all the things he had been called, patient wasn't one of them. Even nurses had found different ways to refer to him.

He had a town to run, a campaign to manage, an election to win, and gates to seal against outsiders; this nomad was wasting time. Pounding the desk, he stood to the full height of his small stature.

"Tell me who, stranger. Who poses us a danger? Psychos in hockey masks? Cannibals? Killer clowns from outer space?"

The nomad hesitated to answer. "Some are, yes. But not the clowns, no, I don't see that happening. That one you made up. But the cannibals, psychos and such, yes."

"Then our walls will keep them out. Until someone can show me proof that our lives our threatened, this town doesn't need a post-apocalyptic nomadic warrior eating its food and preying on its women. The only real threat we have here is strangers coming into town and trying to con us."

The nomad put up his hands in defense. "Okay, okay. That's

great. You say you have no troubles? Fine. Good." Defeated, he stood to leave.

The walls of the metal barn flexed and rumbled at the opening of one of the doors. It boomed even louder when the door shut, announcing the arrival of a beautiful blonde.

Homespun fabric draped her body. It was apparent that someone in town possessed exceptional seamstress skills and this woman displayed them in the best possible way. The light fabric danced about her figure as she crossed the room to the mayor's office. She paid no attention to the two men.

Roy Tinner and the nomad watched her as she walked. The nomad sat back down and started to fill out the form. "Do you have any welding that needs done?"

# 2

———

Graceful until impact, the nomad glided through the air and landed hard on the ground outside the gates of New Hope.

Chin up, chest out, feet arching behind his back to touch, for only a moment, the top of his ears, the landing would have been considered one of the great pratfalls of history had it not caused such pain.

Striking the ground with his face first did little to distribute the force across his body. Forced breath blew dust from the ground as the wind was forced from his lungs. After catching his breath, he began to probe his teeth with his tongue to make sure that all were still present in his face.

Corrugated metal rumbled as the gate to the town bounced across the ground, digging ruts into the dry clay soil of the former North Texas prairie. It closed, rattling one last time as a solid piece of lumber fell into place and sealed him off from the first fresh vegetables, fruit, and meat he had come across in weeks.

The nomad rolled into a sitting position and stretched his jaw back into place. Finding the proper placement for his feet was more difficult than he thought it should have been, but he was able to stand and turn to face the town. Gritty earth fell from his palms as he brushed them together and knocked dirt from the worn fabric of his jacket.

The ringing in his head intensified as he yelled over the wall, "You're going to need a post-apocalyptic nomadic warrior sooner or later!"

"We'll get another one," was the distant reply from the other side of the wall.

It hurt to hear his own voice and for a moment he thought he might be sick, but he yelled back, "Oh, yeah? From where?"

"Hello, Bookworm." The voice was smooth, tempered, and made the nomad wince. He dropped his head and a heavy sigh escaped his lips. The nomad turned to face the man who had addressed him.

"Hello, Logan."

The foundry that was the wasteland had forged many hardened men like Logan. Savage beasts, brutal men, and other dangers had given many a haggard look. Few, however, were able to convert the lacerations, beatings, and hardships into a look such as his.

Hardly disfigurements, his scars wore as accessories instead of detriments. Each scar held a position on the rugged and handsome face that would place it on a wish list for leading men in any action film, rather than on a dermatologist's surgical schedule.

Even this man's clothes had shaped the wasteland's effects to his benefit. From his jacket to his boots, every tear, shred, and burn had the feel of comfortable jeans filled with marks that were stories, not stains. Tales, not tears. Each mark was a treasured memory—each was a chapter of a biography.

Logan's boots were beaten black leather that had never seen a shine and would reject any polish that dared come near the full grain leather. Hundreds of miles had pounded the soles to the point of repair several times over.

He stood, his feet crossed, leaning against the side of a ravaged black Mustang GT that looked not unlike its owner. Sheet metal showed through the faded paint at all points of the car from unfortunate journeys through sandstorms, near misses with debris, and untold battles across the wasteland.

Despite the bashed body panels and rough exterior, a low roar rumbled from the dual exhaust pipes. Even at idle, the engine made its aftermarket work evident as its breathing swirled dust into devils and its power bounced rocks away from the tires.

A dog of indistinguishable breed sat in the passenger seat, disinterested in the conversation.

"Still having trouble convincing people you can help them, I see." Logan placed a hand-rolled cigarette between his lips and lit it with a Zippo that currently used cologne as fuel. Even his lighter smelled manly.

"There's always another town," the nomad said as he continued to dust himself off.

"Give it up, Bookworm. You're not cut out for this line of work."

"I'm not comparing résumés again, Logan. I'm just trying to help people."

"That's what makes us different. You're trying to help people. I am helping people."

"No. What makes us different is that ugly mullet you refuse to get cut."

"Hair jokes? Really?"

"It's no joke, Logan. No amount of nukes could bomb us back far enough in time to make that haircut cool again."

"Don't be petty."

"You're the one trying to be Petty or some other NASCAR driver. I could never tell them apart."

Logan took a long drag and exhaled the smoke before answering. "I'm not doing this with you. I'm here to help the good people of ... Where the hell is this?"

"New Hope."

"Really?"

The nomad nodded. "No marks for originality."

Logan shook his head and chuckled. "Another great new democracy?"

"I've seen greater."

"It doesn't matter. I'm going to help them," said Logan

"They say they don't need any help."

"No, Bookworm. They said they don't need your help. I'm sure they'll listen to me." Logan reached into the Mustang and pulled out a satchel. Its leather was as worn as that of his boots. Slinging it over his shoulder, he whistled to his dog and started moving toward the town gate.

Nails clicked against the sheet metal as the mutt scrambled out of the car and rushed to be at its master's side. Mottled, gray, and missing the top half of one ear, the dog looked as if it had lost as many fights as it had won. It caught up to Logan and strolled at his side as the man strode toward the gate.

As he passed by the nomad, Logan put a hand out and rested it on the man's shoulder.

"I'm serious, Bookworm. You need to find something else to do. This line of work isn't for you. I say that because I care."

"You say that because I'm the competition."

"I say that because of Eternal Hope, Colorado! Do you want to lead more people to their slaughter?"

"Colorado wasn't my fault." It wasn't an argument, but a sheepish reaction, a defensive reflex. He didn't believe it himself.

"I was there. You designed the defenses. You said they would hold." Logan dropped his hand from the nomad's shoulder.

"They should have held."

Logan's voice calmed. "They didn't hold. And we both know what happened next."

Transported back to the courtyard of Eternal Hope, Colorado, the nomad went silent; his eyes went blank. The screams of hundreds surrounded him. Men and women died at his feet. Children pleaded for help as they were carried away.

Acrid smoke had filled his nostrils that day as he screamed commands and struck at everything within his reach. The explosives the raiders had used were crude, but effective at making things explode. Destruction surrounded him; shrapnel had struck his leg and limited his movements. Rage had carried him forward, fighting on, but his efforts could not stop the slaughter.

"You're no warrior, Bookworm. You're a librarian. You don't have what it takes." Logan looked around. "It even looks like your own dog has left you."

The veil of memory lifted. The screams stopped. The nomad's eyes focused. He looked around the area. "Where's Chewy?"

A sharp bang of metal rang out from the town's gate. A yelp carried over the wall. Shouting followed. A low bark was the final sound from inside the town. Metal rumbled like thunder as the town gates scraped open just far enough for a large dog to slip through. The gate slammed shut again.

At 170 pounds and almost three feet tall at the shoulder, it was hard to tell if the giant dog had a piece of lettuce hanging from its jowls or an entire head locked within its jaws.

Regardless, it was pleased with its prize. The canine pranced to the nomad and sat in front of him. Brown eyes stared into his, looking for praise.

Chewy was a mastiff mixed with something brown. She bore the size and stature of her dominant breed, but possessed a thinner jaw line than a purebred mastiff.

"At least your dog got fed."

Chewy turned and growled at Logan—the threatening posture was made less intimidating by the lettuce leaf flapping like a limp flag from her jowls.

The gray mutt at Logan's heel stepped in front of its master. Its hackles were raised. Its teeth gleamed.

"Down, Chewy," the nomad commanded.

The mastiff ceased her growling and sat back down—quiet and content to chew on the lettuce. He placed his hand on the dog's broad head and stroked it, making sure to scratch behind the ears.

"Your dog knows when to quit, Bookworm. You should too. Get out of the game before it kills you."

Logan strolled to the gate and rang the doorbell.

The nomad turned his back to the town of New Hope and, with the mastiff at his side, walked into the wasteland that had been North Texas.

Logan watched the pair walk away as he waited for someone to answer the door. The gray dog continued to growl. Logan made no move to correct the dog.

A loud groan brought his attention back to the gate.

Roy Tinner peered through a crack in the door. "This door isn't light. I'm not opening it without a damn good reason."

"You'll want to see what I have to show you," Logan said.

"I doubt that."

Logan placed a cigarette between his lips and said nothing. The councilman's face hardened. His eyes narrowed—trying to stare down the man outside while struggling to peer through the crack in the gateway.

Logan's face held little expression minus the slight smirk of an upturned corner of his mouth.

A muffled voice came from behind the gate and the man behind the door broke the stare. "It's another one," he said to the muffled voice.

It was a boisterous muffle, but Logan could not distinguish the words being spoken.

"He's probably no different from the last one," Roy responded.

There was more boisterous mumbling and Tinner's expression changed. The scowl disappeared and was replaced with a politician's practiced smile. "Can we help you?"

"No. But I can help you."

Patience had never come easy to the councilman and he had already used what little he had dealing with the fool who was now walking away. His smile disappeared.

"Look, I already did this once today." Roy thrust a thumb at the nomad in the distance. "What the hell do you want?"

"I'm a post-apocalyptic nomadic warrior. And you're going to need my help."

"Look. I'm going to tell you what I told the last nomadic warrior that came through here. We don't have any problems. There aren't any roving gangs. There aren't any sinister people out there looking to do us harm. The biggest problem we seem to have is that the damn doorbell still works." Smiling, he reached out of the gate and hit the button several times.

Logan smirked. It never ceased to amaze him how citizens felt safe behind their walls. Communities had banded together and labored to drive stakes, weld joints and fortify these barriers to feel sheltered, to define themselves as a people set apart from the rest, never realizing for a moment that they were building a prison for themselves.

Explaining this could take hours and result in a slammed door. Today, Logan had no reason to argue.

Without losing the man's gaze, Logan reached into the worn leather satchel and withdrew a cracked and cobbled Flip video camera. Its case was all but shattered; duct tape held it together, as it did so many things in the new world. Spliced wires ran to several batteries that had been bundled together to replace an internal power source that had long since died. The patchwork of wires and Arkansas chrome wasn't an elegant solution, but it worked.

Logan pressed play.

The councilman watched, unmoved. A moment later he tore the device from the man's hands, drawing the tiny screen closer to his face.

"What town is this?"

"This was Vita Nova. Not far from here."

The councilman strained to push the door open farther. "Come in. Bring the camera."

3
_____

"Vita Nova ... sounds nice." The nomad held the map page out for the dog to see.

He had traded a bottle of hydrogen peroxide and an issue of Mad magazine for the worn atlas page when he had come across a scavenger a couple of weeks earlier.

The scavenger had been covered in scabs and sores. The peroxide was what he needed, but he seemed more excited to do the fold in on the back cover of the magazine. Coughing and chuckling, he had scored the page and laughed uproariously when the image revealed itself.

It was a toilet.

Information was not given freely on the road. In a world where so many had so little, everything had become a commodity. Water sources and the location of supplies were the most valuable, if their existence could be verified. The location of towns was not as valuable, but he was still surprised to get the map for such a price.

Only the eastern half of the state was included in the deal; it had been torn from a two-page spread in an old road atlas. By its very nature, any information on the hand-drawn map was suspect, but even general locations would help anyone forced to travel the roads.

Amateur cartography had fallen out of vogue long before the apocalypse, so he was surprised to see that this map's maker had included something as basic as a key. The scraggly drawn box in the corner indicated symbols that had become commonplace in the new world. Like a post-apocalyptic hobo code, scrawled symbols on rocks and roadsides warned travelers of poisoned wells, irradiated areas, and dangerous creature habitats. These symbols had permeated the culture and been spread across the continent by roamers, scavengers, and people that crossed the great wastes in hopes of finding some mythical city that had survived the bombs.

New settlements and unique landmarks were marked by hand: towns, trading posts, radioactive hot spots, and more were hashed onto the old paper. The nomad made a mental note of Vita Nova's location, folded the map, and shoved it back inside his duster.

Chewy barked.

"Well, as nice a place as any."

The massive dog barked again, then whimpered.

"I know. They didn't even let us stay for dinner. At least you got some fresh greens."

He scratched the dog's large square head. This affection was reciprocated with a moist tongue on his fingers.

"Don't worry. There's food in the truck." They had been walking for forty-five minutes and he began to regret parking so far from the town of New Hope. The walled settlement was no longer visible and they still had a fair distance to travel.

It was quiet. Even the ceaseless sounds of the cicadas had ceased. Despite his dog's presence, he felt very much alone.

New Hope was the first real town they had found in weeks. Chewy was a good friend, but it wouldn't hurt to talk to a person about the weather, the apocalypse, or some other manner of small talk.

It was true that almost every city that had not been wiped out during the apocalypse had at least one resident. More times than not it was a crotchety man that refused to leave his home. Years of solitude, however, tended to drive these hermits insane. Insane people made for poor company and were difficult to talk to, as their imaginary friends kept interrupting.

Chewy and the nomad had spent days outside of New Hope before he had mustered the courage to approach the town. He had considered a ruse, posing as a farmer, a douser, a scavenger— anything but a post-apocalyptic nomadic warrior. It would have been easier. Few resisted the help of a skilled douser. But it would not have been honest.

So now it was on to Vita Nova. Another town, another chance to help, and another chance at fresh food and some company.

Distance was no judge of time. It was hard to say how long the trip would take just by looking at the map. Vita Nova wasn't far, but road conditions were unpredictable. Evacuations had been poorly planned and were sporadic at best. This left one to only guess at where the shells of rusting vehicles would be clustered on the roads. Bridges could be out. Barricades could be left intact. It could take a few hours or several days before they reached the town.

Looking west, he determined that it would not be today. Threatening clouds were building in front of the sunset. Winds blew the red dust of the West in front of the coming storm. They would hole up on the road somewhere in a few hours, wait out the storm, and strike out again in the morning.

There was no doubt in his mind that when they arrived at the town, he would find something very similar to the town he had just left: big walls, wary citizens, and a chance at redemption. He could draw a layout of the town, sight unseen, and the sketch would be 90% accurate. All towns were the same.

Parking out of sight, he would approach on foot to appear less threatening to the timid, and less of a target to the bold who saw visitors as a chance to resupply town wares.

This time he wouldn't wear the false confidence. It had failed in New Hope. It wasn't him. He wasn't comfortable with it, and it hadn't gotten him anywhere. No, he would humbly offer his help to the people of Vita Nova and pray that they would accept his offer.

"Come on, Chewy."

The large dog huffed and strolled ahead with a cautious ear to the wasteland. The nomad followed, thankful for his dog's companionship. Having her as a friend made leading a rough life on the road a little easier.

After a moment, he called ahead to her, "Girl, do you remember where we parked the Winnebago?"


It wasn't really a Winnebago. It was a Bounty Hunter motor coach that had been used by off-road enthusiasts before the apocalypse. He rarely felt the need to be brand specific; there weren't many people left alive to argue the difference between the toy hauler and a Winnie.

Motor homes had always fascinated him. Even before the world ended he had dreamed of epic cross-country journeys behind the wheel of a forty-plus-foot land yacht.

He had traveled little growing up, his family always choosing to use vacation time for family reunions, weddings, and other general family visits.

Dubbing these trips as "oblications," he resented the fact that, even after graduating, he felt it necessary to join the family twice a year instead of setting off on his own adventures.

Whenever he passed a large motor coach on the road, his mind wandered to the driver's seat. He saw himself behind the wheel with a map stretched out in front of him. Destinations would dance in his mind. They appeared as postcards and bumper stickers to be earned and pasted with pride on the back of the luxury camper.

Famous landmarks often topped his list: Mount Rushmore, the Mall in D.C., and the Golden Gate Bridge. These and many more filled a hopeless itinerary of places he longed to see. After the apocalypse, he figured it was as good a time as any to get started.

During one of the more severe locust swarms, the two travelers had sought shelter in a storage facility in Oklahoma. The behemoth had been waiting there for them; the keys were hidden behind the visor.

Chewy had claimed the passenger seat for herself and curled up before he had even turned the ignition.

Regret hit him at every stop. Few of the landmarks retained their former beauty. If the apocalypse had not taken its toll on America's greatest treasures, survivors had.

The Golden Gate Bridge had been transformed into the town of Hope Gate. This sprawling shantytown marred the majesty of the former record-holding bridge. Though disappointed, he couldn't fault the people of the town. They had little choice but to settle the span, as most of the land around it had been consumed by the Pacific Ocean.

On the National Mall, someone had stolen the head of Thomas Jefferson, chiseled the beard off of Lincoln, and scrawled "it looks like a penis" on the Washington Monument.

A surviving group of plane fanatics had taken over the Air and Space Museum and spent their days sitting in the cockpits of historic aircraft making machine gun noises and talking about modeling.

Due to the remote location of Mount Rushmore, he had been certain that it would have remained untouched. It was perhaps the greatest disappointment. The once impressive monument had been set upon by a clan of artists that had changed the likenesses of the former presidents into a massive tribute to the Muppets. From left to right were Fozzie, Beaker, Dr. Bunsen Honeydew, and the closest in resemblance, Sam the Eagle.

When he had pressed the artists for a reason for their actions, they simply answered "irony" and attempted to sell him a postcard.

Carved into the granite in the middle of nowhere, he had always assumed that the monument would outlast mankind itself. His hopes dashed, he bought the postcard and a bumper sticker anyway. He never understood the irony.

Traveling the country in the coach had given him ample opportunity to customize the vehicle to the demands of the wasteland. This included an exterior paint job that was designed to hide the massive machine in the shadows.

Matte black paint covered the majority of the motor coach; the chrome bumpers had been removed and replaced with steel rails and brush bars that matched the color scheme. The only exception to the dull exterior was a high-gloss script of the vehicle's christened name, The Silver Lining.

The christening was performed with a 40 of the High Life. He had given the Bounty Hunter the optimistic name before he had set out on his cross-country journey. His plan back then was to spread a little optimism on his tour. Now, he hid the vehicle before approaching any town.

The old service station's canopy had collapsed on one side. This post-apocalyptic lean-to had made the perfect garage. Shadows cast by the dilapidated building blended with the custom matte black paint and helped prevent the coach from being seen by a passing glance.

The pair walked toward it under the beating summer sun. Chewy panted and quickened her pace as the pads of her paws bounced off the hot asphalt. She took refuge under every patch of shade they happened across. A tree or fallen road sign would cause her to run ahead of her master. There she would wait until he caught up.

The nomad had removed his jacket and slung it over his shoulder. His hat was his sole protection from the relentless sun.

"You know what's wrong with this apocalypse, Chewy? It is nothing like anyone expected. Almost everyone is getting along just fine. There's plenty of food, water, and even gasoline isn't worth fighting over."

Fumbling in his pockets, he pulled out two knives and a grenade before hearing the familiar jingle of his keys.

"I shouldn't be complaining. It's good for everyone, right? But it makes doing what we do kind of pointless."

Shuffling from foot to foot, the dog scratched at the door.

"Still, I spent all that time training to fight injustice, to defeat impossible odds, and to drive really fast. Maybe I should have been a farmer. Or I could have been that guy who can build anything out of other things. Everybody likes that guy."

He knelt and reached under the carriage. By habit his fingers found a small metal switch and flicked it off. He stood and placed the key in the door. It resisted and he made note to hit it with some silicone. Dust, dirt, debris, and more were so prevalent in the air that he spent hours each week maintaining the vehicle.

"Let's face it, girl. No one needs a post-apocalyptic nomadic warrior. Especially one like me."

Whimpering, in part out of sympathy, but mostly out of a desire to get inside, his faithful friend nuzzled his hand.

"That's a good girl." He stroked the brindled fur. "At the next town we'll change our vocation. We'll tell them I'm a mechanic. Every town needs one of those. We're getting out of the nomadic warrioring game and we'll settle down for good."

With the hidden switch safely set to off, he opened the door without it exploding.

Chewy brushed by him into the coach and located a bone in the passenger's map pocket. She curled up in the seat and set to work gnawing on the bone.

Fear of knowing the truth had always stopped him from trying to figure out where the bone had originated. It looked like any other bone you would give a dog. But in the world today, there was no telling for sure what kind of animal it had come from. If it had come from an animal at all.

He stepped inside and set the duster on a table. Various clunks sounded as the jacket and the weapons inside settled into place.

Wiping the sweat from his brow, he settled into the cockpit and inserted the keys. The diesel engine turned easily and the motor home purred to life. He placed his hand on the dash just above the vents.

"I missed you, air conditioning."

Chewy sighed in agreement and chomped harder on the bone. There was a crack that sickened the nomad. He pushed the bone's possible origin from his mind.

"Ready, Chewy?"

A steady stream of drool began to flow from her jowls as Chewy worked on the bone.

The nomad held a button on the steering wheel. A chime

sounded throughout the cabin's surround sound system and he spoke. "Play playlist Jerry's favorites."

The iPod beeped a confirmation and played Wonderlust King by Gogol Bordello.

The gypsy punk sound filled the cabin, and the two friends pulled into the afternoon summer sun toward the town of Vita Nova.

# 4

---

"What does Vita Nova mean, anyway?" Roy Tinner sat with Mayor David Wilson and Logan, the post-apocalyptic nomadic warrior, in the mayor's office.

"It's Latin," said the mayor. "It means 'new hope.'"

Roy's eyes widened. "What? They can't do that!"

"Do what?" Logan asked.

"We're New Hope. This is, this is … copyright infringement." Roy stood. "How could they do this? It's an insult, it's an, an affront."

"An affront?" Logan looked to the mayor.

"Calm down, Roy," he said, barely acknowledging the pacing councilman as he mulled over the warrior's story and what he had seen on the camera.

"They can't …" Roy stammered when he was agitated. He stammered often.

"They're dead," Logan said. "Your pending lawsuit isn't going to be their biggest concern."

Roy stopped pacing. His cheeks flushed, he sat back down. The gravity of the situation had escaped him in his offense. He stammered, "Of course. Still, we should see to preventing this in the future."

Logan walked over to a large map on the wall, grabbed a pen and started marking towns and settlements. With each dot he proclaimed the name of the location. "Hope, Hopeful, Last Hope, Hopefulville, The Town of New Hopefulvilleness, The Town of Hope, Hope City, New Hope, New Hope, New Hope ..."

Tinner winced with each location and squirmed in his chair. New Hope was the name he had championed during the drafting of the town's charter. The moniker had faced stiff competition from Freedonia and Freedomville. Political favors and pure begging had helped him force his choice through.

"The world is full of Hopes, Mr. Tinner." Logan set the marker back down.

"They're all Hope?"

"I came across a Steve once."

"Steve?"

"They figured it sounded warm and welcoming, because 'Who doesn't like Steve?'"

Roy nodded, but then added, "Why not Steven?"

Logan shrugged. "Too pretentious?"

"I don't know. I knew a few Stevens, seemed nice enough."

The mayor jumped in, "Please, Roy. It's not important right now."

Tinner dropped the issue, but decided that his first act as the new mayor would be to change the name of the town. A new flag would be needed as well. He decided to start sewing one up that night.

Mayor Wilson sat, his head propped on his fingertips. Pensive, he stared not at Roy Tinner or Logan, but into the wall beyond them both.

The video was disturbing. Horrific. The news that a similar fate could await his town had removed the ever-present, reassuring smile he had adopted since the apocalypse.

Dozens of people looked to him for guidance and assurances that —even though the world had come to an end—everything would be okay. Men and women had come from all over to this town to be safe and, for the first time, the mayor wasn't certain that he could promise that safety.

"Well, this isn't good." The mayor looked to Logan and indicated the Flip. "How old is this footage?"

"Yesterday. I arrived not long after the assault. Too late to help, unfortunately."

"And you're sure that they are headed this way?"

Logan shrugged. "They were headed south. New Hope is the next inhabited town."

"So they could be here any moment." The mayor stood and walked to the map of Texas that hung on the wall. Logan had drawn in the approximate location of Vita Nova just across the former state line.

"We should evacuate." Roy Tinner was two steps toward the door. "I'll have everyone start rounding up the supplies."

"Hold on." Logan raised a hand to stop the councilman and turned back to the mayor. "You may have a few days. This entire road is lined with deserted towns." Logan indicated the route on the map. "They won't pass them up—no matter how fierce they are, they're scavengers at heart. And, with any luck, the road may prove difficult for them."

"What do you propose?" The mayor was hesitant to abandon the town, but for once he thought he may agree with Tinner.

"Your walls are strong. Some of the strongest I've seen. With a few modifications and some arms for the town, you'd be able to make a stand here."

"Is that what Vita Nova did?" Roy had picked up the Flip and replayed the footage. "Evacuation is our only chance. And, if we leave, they'll just pass by when they find nothing here. Then we can come back."

"Or, they'll track you down and you won't have a wall to hide behind."

"No, Roy," Mayor Wilson turned his back to the map on the wall. "New Hope is where other people go when they need help. This is our home and we will defend it."

"David, this is a bad idea."

The mayor nodded. He couldn't completely disagree with the councilman. Defending the town may be the biggest mistake he would make during his career as mayor. This was little consolation in the fact that it could also be his last.

"It could be, Roy. But it's the right thing to do."

"You're putting us in danger."

"Danger is being put upon us, Roy. Don't think for a moment that I'm forgetting what's at stake here. My daughter's is one of the lives I'm putting on the line. But I would rather stand and fight and show her that true freedom is worth defending, than run and most likely be killed anyway.

"We've worked too hard to build this town to abandon it to the will of savages and bullies."

The mayor stood and offered his hand to the warrior. "This isn't your fight, I know. Still, is there any way I could convince you to stay and help us?"

Logan looked to Roy. The fat man perspired in anticipation of the warrior's answer.

"Help us prepare our defense," the mayor continued, "and you can take with you all the supplies you can carry."

"I'll help. But I don't want anything."

"Then why would you ...?"

"I have my reasons."

"David," Roy's voice bordered on rage, "we can defend ourselves."

"Every hand helps," the mayor looked back to Logan.

Logan nodded, "I'll survey the town and start making plans."

"Again, thank you."

"I'm not going to let you do this, David. Not like this. You'll have to take this to the council."

Mayor Wilson nodded. "Of course, you're right. We'll take this to the people. Mr. Logan, would you mind addressing the council?"

"If it will help."

Roy stammered something unintelligible, stormed out of the office, and slammed the door. The steel walls of the barn rattled a moment later as Roy slammed the outer door.

"He doesn't like outsiders," said Logan. "That's his problem, isn't it?"

"No," said the mayor. "He's an asshole. And it's more our problem than his."

Logan tried not to smirk. He couldn't do it.

"By the way, Logan. Do you play kickball?"

# 5

Roads weren't much worse than before the world's nations had seen fit to drop bombs all over them. With the exception of a few biological agents, it was rare that warheads contained anything that promoted the growth of plant life, or any life.

Vegetation had survived, but its growth had seemed stunted and easily held at bay by the existing concrete or asphalt barriers. Road surfaces would crumble in time, but for now they stayed smooth where they had been smooth, rough where they had been rough, and shitty all throughout Arkansas.

Traveling in the large coach had its benefits, large shock absorbers being one of them. Jerry had made extensive alterations to the motor coach, but he had seen little need to modify the suspension.

Other modifications were more crucial.

Larger water reservoirs ensured hydration in the wastelands and the poisoned areas of the country. Solar panels and battery racks powered essential emergency systems that included the halogen bars that blinded light sensitive mutations. A beer fridge kept his beer cold.

A large plasma screen TV had been discarded in favor of turning its retractable housing into a weapons rack. Here he kept the majority of his larger weapons: assault rifles, shotguns, and a couple of submachine guns that he had come across over the years.

The second plasma screen was still in place and was hooked to a DVD, VCR, and extensive sound system. Lining a media shelf nearby were the essential reference materials for those in his line of work. The DVD collection was comprehensive, including everything from *A Boy and His Dog* to *Zardoz*.

Everything that he and Chewy could need in the new world was carried in the Silver Lining. It provided the perfect post-apocalyptic existence; diesel was easy enough to make and the head was easy enough to dump.

Often, he felt like a cheat. No post-apocalyptic nomadic warrior in any pre-apocalyptic film or fiction had traveled in such luxury. Most traveled on foot or in a beat-up muscle car. Custom military transports were the ideal mode of transportation, but they were the exception, even in Hollywood.

The Silver Lining was practical. He always argued with himself that if he was better prepared, he could be a better ally to those in need. Besides, it was better to be a rested post-apocalyptic nomadic warrior that slept in a queen-sized bed, than one with lower back pains from a bedroll and rocky ground.

Chewy snored. Her face mushed against the window, drool streaked down the glass, collected on her mighty paw, spilled over, and dripped into the map pocket, collecting in a disgusting pool at the bottom.

Sunlight faded behind oncoming storm clouds, pulling the world into a darkness that it had not known since before Edison's epiphany. Jerry made no move to turn on the lights. Instead, he reached into a console beside him and pulled out a pair of night vision goggles and strapped them over his head.

Using lights was iffy at best.

While the halogen system on the roof of the vehicle was installed to repel mutants with sensitive eyes, it tended to attract others with less squinty vision. Clouds of mutant insects could descend upon the coach in swarms so thick that all forward motion would be a ding-filled game of gas-and-bump.

Rain lashed against the windshield moments later. Sheets of off-colored water flooded his line of sight. The wipers did little to fight off the downpour. Static filled the goggles. At first the haze was light, but as the rain grew thicker, the lenses displayed only white snow. He removed them and signaled to pull to the side of the road.

Cursing, he hit the signal lever to turn it off. It went too far and the left blinker engaged. He slapped it back down. The right blinker began again. Left, right, left, and then off. He grunted.

Relieved that the signals had gone unnoticed, he chuckled to himself that, after several years of being one of the only vehicles on the road, he still signaled before pulling the Silver Lining to the shoulder and parking it along the curb.

Outwardly he laughed, but he knew that it was small things like this that gave him hope for humanity's resurgence. If we can remember to use a blinker, he thought to himself, we'll remember everything else.

He cut the engine and stared into the darkness outside the windshield. Pulses of distant lightning illuminated the roadside. Something caught his eye, even though he couldn't make out what the object was. He moved into the passenger seat and forced his face into the corner of the windshield. He waited for another strike.

Most highway signs had been blown over or salvaged for shelters, but not ten feet from where he had stopped one had been replaced. It had been propped up with a variety of wood and steel poles. The messaging had been altered. Fluorescent orange paint covered the exit number, but other words had been added: Vita Nova, food, drink, shelter, and hope. The final word was painted the largest.

"Looks like we found it, Chewy."

The large dog broke wind and startled herself. Her head snapped around and she looked at her master.

"It wasn't me. You farted."

She didn't buy it.

The smell filled the cabin.

"Oh, Chewy." He moved quickly into the back of the coach. The odor followed him. "I can't even open a window."

Chewy got up and moved to the door. She began to paw at the latch.

"We can't. It's metal rain." That's what people called it anyway. It struck hard and stung like flecks of metal. It crashed on steel and tin with a clatter that led one to believe it would cut right through. Plus, the name reminded people of the '80s.

The truth was nobody knew what was in the precipitation, but the common perception was that if it hurt like hell and caused electrical interference, it was best to stay out of it.

Chewy's bowels were not aware of this. She whimpered and began to huff. These small huffs from the large dog sent drool flying across the motor coach.

"You know we can't go outside."

The dog began to whine.

"No. You're going to have to hold it."

She snorted, then stepped from her seat and into the rear cabin. It was not a pleasant night for either of them.


Jerry was aware that Vita Nova was Latin for New Hope, but after spotting the town from a distance, he could tell that the name didn't fit. Hope appeared to be as scarce as everything else in town. There was no activity. No movement.

"That sign was false advertising, Chewy." He scanned the walled town through powerful binoculars.

"I don't see anything. There's nothing going on there."

He placed the binoculars in the case and climbed down the side of the Silver Lining to where the dog sat staring up at him.

"Still, we should check it out. At the very least they could have some fresh supplies."

A bark of agreement set the dog on all fours, ready to greet new people and smell new things.

"I'll have to change."

One errant prediction about the apocalypse was that all retail and clothing warehouses would be destroyed and all humanity would resort to wearing patchwork robes and parts of old tires. Worst-case situations had forced some to wear homespun garments, but with a little planning, most colonies could send a team out to shop the racks of former malls, strip centers, or neighborhoods. With 97 percent of the world's population no longer needing them, closets full of clothes were up for grabs.

For some, the homemade clothes were a choice. Many towns had settled as isolationists. Fear compelled them to live within their walls, venturing beyond only in the direst of situations. Visitors to these communities were under constant supervision, if they were permitted entry at all.

Others had taken a more wary approach to post-apocalyptic life and committed themselves to living off the land. Blaming technology and man's materialism for the downfall of humankind, they chose to revert to a more simplistic existence.

Towns like these never lasted long in the face of opposition. Primitive towns were also the most reluctant to accept assistance, if that assistance came with guns or machines. Some of these settlements, though only seven years from the apocalypse, had taken to referring to technology as witchcraft for the benefit of their children. Such language was to ensure that future generations would not become enamored with the trinkets of man's destruction.

Jerry wore a broken-in pair of Levi's and a Captain America T-shirt he had pulled off the shelf at an Old Navy. The Silver Lining's wardrobe held several changes of comfortable clothes that lacked tears, stains, or dirt. However, these gave the wrong impression when acting in the capacity of a warrior of the wasteland. Even if he was wrong about the settlement Vita Nova was, it was best to never knock on a gate overdressed.

There was no need to pull a Michelin off of the spare tire rack and cut it into shoulder pads or a crotch strap, but when approaching a new town, appearances needed to be maintained. He stepped into the coach and pulled open the wardrobe.

Task-specific clothes were kept in storage under the floor—winter wear, desert survival equipment, protective gear, even a radiation suit—but the wardrobe held everyday wear. T-shirts, jeans, and a couple of flannels hung beside his work clothes.

The plan had not changed. He would introduce himself as a post-apocalyptic nomadic mechanic. But, with little sign of motion from the town, he thought it best to be prepared for trouble. His outfit was that of a drifter. Mechanics could be drifters, he reasoned. He didn't want to show up at the gates in coveralls to find that he should have packed his weapons.

Hanging at the end of the closet was a pair of jeans that was more worn than the rest. He pulled these on and stepped into a beaten pair of motorcycle boots. A gray linen pullover covered his T-shirt. He tousled his hair while draping a pair of leather safety goggles around his neck, and tossed the duster over the passenger seat.

He settled back into the driver's seat. Chewy jumped into the seat next to him. Jerry smiled and scratched the big dog on the head. "Today's the day we change our lives, girl."

Chewy slumped over and went to sleep.

He started the coach and they drove to within a mile of the town before parking behind what had once been a Dairy Queen. This led to a brief recollection of Blizzards that ended when he tried to explain to the dog how they would always invert the dessert before it was handed over. Chewy was disinterested and tried to go back to sleep.

Jerry shrugged at his companion's indifference and pulled open a hatch in the floor. Two nickel-plated automatics sat inside. The distinctive .45s served two purposes. One, they were impossible to miss and hard to forget, ensuring that he left a mark in the minds of the town's people. Two, they were match quality .45s, ensuring that he left large holes in the minds of things that attacked him.

Tarnish-free, the pistols reflected the broken light that fell through the dirty windshield, amplified it, and released it back into the world. Each pistol sat on a hip with an empty chamber, safety on.

He pulled the duster over his shoulders and pulled a shotgun from the coat closet next to the door. He slung it around his neck and let it hang across his back.

"Ready, girl?"

Chewy climbed from the passenger seat, yawned, stretched, and moved to his side without enthusiasm. She half huffed, half woofed her reluctance to going outside.

He opened the door. Once exposed to the air, Chewy became excited, broke heel and darted past him, colliding with his knee. He spun and grabbed the counter to steady himself.

"Dammit, Chewy."

# 6

Gregory Emerson swore as he struck his head on the collapsed roof of a Nissan Pathfinder. He rubbed his head as he examined the item that had prompted him to stick his head into the wreckage in the first place.

The frames were bent, but the lenses were thick and free of cracks and scratches. He held the glasses up to his eyes. Instantly, a headache began to creep from the top of his spine to his temples.

"Shit, Magoo. I'll bet you got teased a lot."

He blew on the glasses to clear the dust and a bit of rotting flesh that had stuck in the bridge. Pawing through the wallet, he tossed aside cash and credit cards. These were useless; but if the driver had a condom in there, it was as good as a drink in the next town. He held out the driver's license and chuckled.

"Sorry, Mr. Jenkins. Looks like you were an organ donor. If it makes you feel any better, your nerd glasses will help someone see again. And help me get a meal."

Emerson moved across the massive pileup that had occurred several years before. Climbing to the top of an overturned FedEx truck, he surveyed the field of twisted metal. Giddy, he made his way toward a minivan/F-150 combination.

"Virgin ground. Virgin ground." He danced towards the mash-up of family vehicle and work truck.

The expansive traffic accident had remained untouched since the end of the world. Every vehicle he peered into held a trove of personal belongings that had been gathered in haste for an evacuation that saved no one.

His best guess was that The Creep had been the end of the gridlocked evacuees. A viscous blue fog, The Creep had been a surprise to even the military. Not quite a fog, not quite a liquid, this plasma weapon blew like a tumbleweed across landscapes.

Those unfortunate enough to be downwind of the eerie blue vapor would become enraged and impatient. Lashing out at others, many who had been stuck in traffic turned the crowded roads into demolition derbies. This continued until they were killed in the crashes or succumbed to The Creep itself.

Patches of the notorious weapon still drifted across the landscape as if refusing to dissipate. Prolonged exposure would cause death. Even those caught in a high wind, whether man or animal, would become clouded with rage.

Only the insanity resulting from exposure could explain the pileup. No order could be made of its severity or its location on the otherwise empty stretch of highway. Emerson guessed that they might have even been moving in a caravan since many of the vehicles seemed well supplied.

This mother lode could keep him in business for years. Provided he could keep the cache's location a secret.

He shoved his head through the passenger door of the minivan and checked out the occupants. At least the family had been together when the end came. The family of four had piled the van full of belongings. He would get to all of them in time, but he always went for the glasses first. Their size and weight made them easy to carry, and corrective lenses were prized commodities. This combination made glass picking one of the most profitable professions in the new world.

The dad had contacts or 20/20 vision. Gregory found this disappointing, but he delighted in finding designer rims on Mom.

The scavenger pulled at the frames. What was left of her flesh held them fast to her head and he had to tug to remove them from her face.

A quick glance through the glass confirmed that they weren't bifocals. Single prescriptions were easier to trade. When trading in bifocals you had to find that special someone whose sight matched the previous owner. Nearsighted was nearsighted; single prescription lenses could aid a wider range of customers. If they needed bifocals, he would just sell them two pair instead of one.

He checked for wedding rings next.

Gold was everywhere now, but he firmly believed that soon it would be valued as currency again. No age in recorded history had seen the metal worthless and he knew that history was due to repeat itself. When it did, he would be one of the richest men in the new world.

Two children in car seats stared back at him from the back seat, their gaze empty. A Texas Rangers ball cap covered the little boy's head; in his hand was a baseball mitt. Shreds of a pink dress were the only indication that the other child was a little girl. Grasped in her arm was a blue-hued teddy bear. Decay had robbed her body of muscle, but the grip on her beloved toy was unmistakable.

Blue mold had grown on the toy's fur, but still, the bear looked familiar to him. He looked back at the driver and to the mother in the passenger seat, viewing the bodies as people for the first time in years.

Gregory Emerson had scavenged countless bodies in the past seven years. What he found, he traded for necessities and luxuries. He made a better living in the aftermath than he had before the world blew up, but it had hardened his nerves, robbed him of a conscience, and, with each profitable trade, he had swapped a little more of his humanity. Over the years, empathy had left him a piece at a time. Now, it rushed back to him in an instant.

Tears filled his eyes as he backed out of the minivan. Deep breaths could not fill the pain in his lungs as he wiped the dirt from the designer glasses. Sputtering, his nose began to drip. Tears flooded his vision. Sobs shook his entire body, but he reached back into the passenger window and placed the glasses back on his sister's face.

Collapsing to the ground, he drew his knees to his chest as the salt of the tears filled his mouth.

"I'm sorry," he cried to no one and everyone. He stood and began to scream at the decaying drivers around him, "I'm sorry! I'm sorry you're all dead. It sucks. It sucks and I wish I could make it all go away."

He sputtered as he spoke.

"I wish I could just wave my hand and make it all go away!" He swept his hand at the pileup. At the distant end of the massive wreck, two cars went flying into the air.

It rumbled, turning sod to dust as it plowed across the shoulder and onto the road. Desolate cars long abandoned were thrust from its path by the steel plow mounted to the grill of the armor-clad semi.

Black with a blood red band down its crest, diesel smoke belched from the extended stacks as the truck barreled down the road. Every part of the truck had been blacked out. Its matte finish absorbed the daylight, swallowing it whole and giving nothing back.

The rig hauled four trailers; two tandem pairs rumbled side by side. This configuration consumed both lanes of the blacktop from shoulder to shoulder and formed a moving wall of darkness.

Jagged teeth lined the plow in front of the truck. The metal barricade extended well beyond the cab and stretched wider than the width of the trailers. On each side of the cab, housed behind the thick-gauged metal of the plow itself, machine gun turrets were poised for action. A gunner in each turret kept vigilant watch from behind thick, tinted goggles and twin .50 caliber machine guns.

More firepower was positioned on top of the trailers. Parapets lined the trailers and men brandishing assault rifles and combat shotguns paced behind them. Each gunner was well trained and ready to discourage any attacker by killing them to great degrees.

The great machine belched huge plumes of smoke as it guzzled homemade diesel fuel and accelerated to clear a small hatchback from its path.

Steel twisted as the Honda's frame collapsed upon itself. The car shot from the road, leaving shattered glass and rusted panels to be crushed by the truck. Rolling end over end, the small car fell apart as bolts loosened and snapped. Peeling body panels littered the ground as it crashed to a stop in the field to the side of the road.

The rig's sleeper cabin had been gutted and converted into a command center. Maps covered with hand-drawn notations hung from the walls. Binders lined spot-welded shelves. Inside each was information on fuel levels, food stores, and ammo stockpiles.

A table stood in the center of the small room. There, a man pored over a manifest, making notations in a spiral bound notebook.

"There's a pileup up ahead, sir. All lanes blocked."

"All stop." Nails, gravel, and shards of glass shaken in a tin can made a more pleasant sound than the voice that came from the man in charge. His skin was like leather, but pale. Lines worn into the face from years of hardship did little to cast shadows. Even the contrast against shock white hair failed to give the skin color. Only the black patch across his eye gave his features definition.

Mechanical systems popped and hissed as the rear air brakes triggered and brought the brute of a vehicle to a stop.

"Get the crew on it. I want the road cleared as soon as possible." The commander's voice was calm, quiet, and terrifying. "I'll be in my cabin."

"Yes, Major."

The commander disappeared from the cab through a fabricated connector that led to the trailers.

The navigator spoke into an intercom on the dash.

"Wrecking detail, dismount."

The command echoed through the trailers of the goliath. Men burst into action. Hidden panels burst open and armored men took up position on the roadside. Each held a rifle and peered down the sights as officers began to give the all clear.

Several more men stepped from the truck brandishing pry bars, steel posts, torches, axes, and more. They set upon the wreckage, prying, bashing, and busting apart the mangled vehicles.

Emerson saw the team emerge from the truck. Dressed in black, they wore the first uniforms he had seen since the bombs fell, the gases hissed, and the bugs were released.

Not long after everything went to hell, there had been rumors that the government had been evacuated safely to Cheyenne Mountain and other shelters. Many had been hopeful that they would return. Others blamed the government for whatever it was that had happened. Either way, after seven years, there had been no sign of the United States of America.

Gregory had always fallen into the second camp. He damned the government for all he had lost and cursed them for hiding like cowards in a hole in the ground, waiting for the suffering to end before reclaiming the country.

Finding his sister's family had changed all of that in an instant. Deep within him welled a longing for order. A longing for the world he had known. He wanted everything to go back to the way it used to be.

These men must be the government. Governments offered stability, order, and from the looks of it, matching uniforms. He wanted no part of his former life as a scavenger. He craved the order of civilization and a chance to make amends.

He climbed to the top of a rusting sedan and waved. "God Bless America!"

Sparks brushed his pant leg as a bullet ricocheted into the wasteland.

"Don't move." The booming voice came from a sound system on the rig.

"Okay!"

Within minutes he was brought before the truck. They had all but stripped the clothes from his body. He had never been so thoroughly frisked without trading a substantial amount for the pleasure.

A guard held him under each arm, while a third kicked at his knees to keep him off of his feet. They dragged him before an open doorway at the side of a trailer.

He protested, "Guys, it's okay. I'm happy to see you."

No response came from the guards.

A man with white hair appeared a moment later. His massive build filled the doorframe.

"What's this?"

"A scavenger, Major," one of the guards said.

"What's your name?"

Emerson hesitated. Any enthusiasm he held waned in the presence of this man with an eye patch. Instinct told him to stand and run, but the guards continued to hold his arms and knock his feet from under him.

"Emerson ... sir."

"Where are you coming from, Everson?"

"I'm from Michigan originally ..."

The major stepped from the trailer and approached the captive. "Michigan. Really?" He held up his right hand and pointed to the open palm. "Which part?"

Gregory smiled and began to point towards the open palm to indicate his hometown.

The palm came crashing down with such speed that Gregory Emerson flinched well after it had struck him.

Blood rushed to the surface of his skin and he felt the sting on his cheek.

"Where were you last, Eberson?" The major held his hand up again, not as a map, but as incentive to answer quickly.

"Uh, New Hope. About a week ago."

"Where is it?"

"Five days, that way." He shrugged. "On foot. About ten miles off the highway."

The major nodded and stepped back into the trailer. A guard closed the door behind him.

The guard behind him stopped kicking at his knees and drew a pistol. Gregory Emerson didn't see the gun. He didn't feel the bullet. Then, he felt nothing at all.

The door opened again and the major reemerged. "Another thing, Everman ..." He looked at the body on the ground. "Why is this man dead?"

"You nodded, sir," the guard with the smoking gun responded.

"So?"

"Well, usually when you nod, it means kill something."

"Yes, but I didn't think you'd be so quick about it." The major stepped from the trailer and stood over the body of Gregory Emerson.

"I ... I don't know what to say."

"I figured you'd at least drag him to the side of the road. I mean, look at this! You got blood and brain all over the truck."

"I'm sorry ..."

"You had better hope this comes out." The major pulled the guard closer, grabbed the man's sleeve, and tried to rub the blood from the black paint of the trailer. He succeeded only in smearing it around. Dropping the guard's arm, he yelled, "Get this cleaned up and get rid of that body."

"Yes, sir."

"And from now on, when I nod, yes, kill something, but take it away and kill it."

"Yes, sir." The guard signaled to the others to dispose of the body as he set to spitting at the splatter on the trailer.

"Not like that, get some water. Take it out of the prisoners' rations."

"Yes, sir."

The guard hurried off as the major yelled after him.

"I want this road cleared STAT. We're heading to New Hope." He stepped back into the trailer and shut the door.

The wrecking crew, having stopped to witness the execution, returned to their task.

Coordinated as their efforts were, the pileup was extensive. Wrecks of rusted cars were twisted together as one. Torches, jackhammers, and more would take days to clear the wreckage. A respect for the dead would cost them weeks. This would not be a factor.

Sparks flew as they began their work.

# 7

———

"What do they want?"

"Food, provisions, men, women, and children."

"Women and children?"

"They're collecting slaves. They kill most of the men and place the women and children in this trailer here." Logan pointed to a crude illustration of the rig that he had sketched on the wall of the town hall barn.

Gasps came from the gathered crowd. Every citizen of New Hope was in attendance to hear the proposed plans for the defense or evacuation of New Hope.

"What do they do with the slaves?" The question arose from the back of the room.

Logan shook his head, "I don't know. Trade them? Forced labor? Worse? There are no limits to this man's evil."

"How many men on this truck?" Sheriff Willie Deatherage looked up at the crude drawing of the rig.

"Twenty or more."

"I'm pretty sure we've got that many bullets."

Logan raised a hand to calm the lawman. "All of them are well armed and trained. They may be former military."

"I don't buy it." A young councilman stood in the back of the room. After speaking with Logan, the mayor had requested a gathering of the town's administrators. Most of the council members supported his plan. Timothy Simmons, however, had been swayed by Roy's arguments. The young council remained skeptical that there was a threat at all.

Simmons pushed a pair of ill-fitting glasses farther up the bridge of his nose before he spoke. "It's been seven years. Seven years since everything stopped and we've never seen anything like this. Why, all of a sudden, is the post-apocalypse turning into Mad Max?"

Logan straightened. "I don't mean to argue, but you've been fortunate. Gangs have formed and towns have burned. I've seen it. And I've stopped it from happening."

"Bullshit. Bullshit, Mr. Logan." The glasses slid back down his nose.

"Why would I make this up?"

"A good question, Mr. Logan. Let's examine that, shall we?" The young councilman approached the front of the room, adjusted his glasses and spoke to the crowd. "Have you ever heard of the grasshopper and the ants?"

Logan shook his head in disbelief. "That's hardly—"

"The ants, ladies and gentlemen, worked diligently all year harvesting food for winter."

Someone in the crowd muttered, "We know the story, Timothy."

The young man continued, fidgeting with his new glasses as he spoke. "They worked hard, storing food so that they might live. But, the grasshopper ..." He turned to face Logan. "The Grasshopper, Mr. Logan, played and played. And he didn't do shit for work."

"Yes, sir. I know the parable and—"

"And when winter came, the grasshopper began to starve. That lazy, lazy grasshopper. And the ants took pity and fed him. No, wait. That's not right."

"I think the ants let him starve," said the Director of Internal Communications.

"No, they fed him and he learned to work hard," said the Secretary of the Treasury.

The crowd began to offer their own recollections of the story.

"I thought that the grasshoppers were bullies."

"No, that was A Bug's Life."

"Was that the one with Stallone?"

"No, that was Ant Bully."

"Antz."

"What?"

"You mean Antz. With a z. Antz."

"What's with a z?"

"The ant movie with Stallone and Woody Allen."

"Look at the movie nerd."

"Shut it, Miller."

"The point is, ladies and gentlemen," Timothy shouted, "that the story is no less true today than when Dr. Seuss first penned it. And here," he pointed to Logan, "is our grasshopper. Knocking on our ant hill with a story about a truck full of killers."

The room was quiet. All men and women looked to Logan. The only sound was Miller and the movie nerd trading insults back and forth. Logan waited for the arguing to stop before he responded.

"Wow. Just, wow. I don't know what to say to that."

"That's what I thought," Timothy began to walk back to his seat.

"Aesop, not Seuss, Mr. Timothy, was a wise man. And," he gestured to a gray-haired man in the front row, "you were right, the ants let the grasshopper starve. And deservedly so. The grasshopper sang and played while the ants toiled. He offered nothing.

"I'm no grasshopper. I offer something. If it is just a warning that a big truck full of killers is headed your way ... fine. You can choose to ignore it, or prepare for it on your own. It doesn't matter to me. But I am offering to stay and help. And not for your winter stores. I don't want anything."

"Then why would you help?"

"Because I used to be an ant." He shifted his feet and choked back a hard memory. "And grasshoppers took everything from me. Good people of New Hope, I see potential in this new world. The blight of mankind's evil was not wiped from this Earth with everything else. But from what's left, there is the hope that a town such as yours can be the model for the new world. It is a good town. A town ruled by the people. Good people.

"And now you are in the path of a force ruled by fear. The two will collide. Whichever is left standing will shape the world to come.

"There is a grasshopper out there and I can't let this be a world created by grasshoppers. I want to live in a world of ants. I want to side with you and protect your way of life. Our way of life."

The crowd was silent, but he could see that his words had moved them. Timothy Simmons saw it as well and sank into his seat. Logan was confident that he could speak without protest.

"I don't want anything from you. I just want to help. Now, I'm going to need some things. We don't have much time."

"How much time do we have?" the sheriff pointed back at the truck.

"We can't be certain. I made the drive from Vita Nova in under a day. They'll take a little longer."

"Why is that?"

"The roads aren't clear enough for a rig of this size. They don't have the luxury of crossing medians. They'll have to make their own path."

# 8

Ash that had been Vita Nova shifted beneath his boots as he moved slowly through the town. Patches of the ground were warm beneath his feet as they stirred the coals of a devastating blaze. An odor hung in the air; it smelled like a campfire that had melted a pair of sneakers.

Frames of the buildings still stood, but they were charred and brittle like burnt matchsticks. Bodies lay everywhere. Some burned beyond recognition, others untouched by the flames. There was nothing left in the town but death and a tricycle.

The little red tricycle lay on its side; one wheel spun from the rising heat of the town. He didn't see the child that once rode it. He didn't want to.

Wasteland travels had exposed him to horrific creatures. Mutant animals hunted for prey with a ferocity and viciousness that no creature had been capable of prior to the bombs.

However, only man could create destruction such as this. Men with a cruelty that rivaled those who had unleashed the apocalypse itself. Only man, or really, really smart bears, could treat living creatures with such malice.

The squeak of the tricycle's wheel slowed and stopped. Apart from the occasional crack of a weakened structure, the town was silent except for a single sound.

Weeping.

"Hello?" The ash soaked up his voice as it swirled around him, driven by a light wind. He yelled louder, "Hello?"

He must have been heard, because the weeping stopped. Footing was hard to find on the ash, but he ran to where he thought the sound had originated. Slipping on the char and coals of the town, he tripped several times. Often he had to put his knee down to maintain his balance. Through his jeans he could feel that parts of the ground were still warm.

Despite the hazardous landscape, he risked twisted or broken ankles to find the source of the crying. Every step stirred a plume of smoke from the ground.

"It's okay to come out. I'm not a threat." He slung the shotgun across his back as he slowed his pace. "I want to help."

There was no response but popping cinders from the town.

"Chewy, find them."

The mastiff barked and began to sniff the air. She traced the scent into the shell of a building and began to smell the ground. Ash and smoke clouded her nose and she began to sneeze.

"You're worthless, you know that?"

The mighty dog barked in disagreement and resumed her hunt. Taking shorter breaths, she overcame the tickling ash and made her way across the town's courtyard to a small metal shed that had been spared by the blaze. Darting inside, she left behind a cloud of ash and a trail of excited chirps.

Jerry followed across the courtyard and came to the door of the shed just as Chewy emerged with a can of chili in her mouth. Drool coated the faded Wolf Brand label.

"Chewy, I said find them, not get dinner."

The massive dog dropped the can of chili at his feet and stared at him.

"No."

She whimpered.

"No. Find the person crying."

The dog snorted and resumed her search. She disappeared behind the shed.

Jerry bent over and picked up the chili. It was cool to the touch despite the hot drool. The shed must lead to a cellar. It could hold stores of food and would be worth checking into once they found whoever had been crying.

"Don't move, you bastard." The woman's voice came from behind him. There was nothing in her tone that signaled she had been crying. He feared that he had walked into a trap.

The duster covered his .45s. He lowered his chili-free hand towards the pistol while turning to face the woman.

"I said don't move. Turning is moving." Her voice sounded like it was coming from behind a rifle. Or a stick.

"Are you okay?" He stretched his hands out, away from his weapons.

"Shut up." Her voice began to shake. So did the rifle.

"What happened here?"

"Everybody died." There it was. The sob he had heard earlier entered her voice.

"I want to help." Slowly, imperceptibly he began to bend at his knees. The duster hid the slight movements from her view.

"Then stand right there and let me shoot you."

"I'm sure there's something else I can do."

"Fine. Who needs your help? I'll do it myself."

"Enough people have died here. Let me help you."

On his right was a brick wall. It was close. Close enough maybe. If he could get enough bend in his knee there was a chance he could spring behind it.

"I'll help myself." There were tears in her voice.

If it threw off her aim enough, her sobbing might just save his life. He considered provoking the tears. Several things came to mind that he could say to encourage her hysterics: "Who did you lose?" "Was he/she a good person?" "But you survived. That's gotta make you feel pretty bad." "Sucks to be you."

He dismissed these as risky and just plain cruel.

She slid the bolt back on the rifle. A large round entered the chamber.

He dove as hard as he could and almost landed behind the brick wall.

The shot erupted a plume of ash where he had stood moments before.

He scrambled to get behind the wall, but he had landed face first in the ash. Soot filled his eyes causing them to water. Blinking frantically, he wiped at his eyes with the backs of his hands and succeeded in making his vision worse.

She worked the bolt.

He dove.

She fired.

The world went black.

# 9

Before the apocalypse, there was a certain dignity in having a quiet drink in one's office. The day's work accomplished, laid out before you, and a shot of bourbon or whiskey was a celebration of a job well done.

Mayor David Wilson realized that all the dignity was lost when drinking a batch of grain alcohol—made in the town's spare bathtub —from a Gerber baby food jar.

He slammed the empty bottle on the desk and looked at the next one. Baby Bogey stared up at him from the metal lid—judging him.

Damn that baby, he thought as he uncapped and downed the shot in one fluid motion. The jar clanged on the desk next to the previous one, setting off a chain reaction of chimes from the empty jars before him.

For seven years there was no celebration at the end of the day. If everyone was alive, it was a job well done. However, the daily task of presiding over the wellbeing of dozens of lives was taking its toll.

Now, it seemed that the citizens' wellbeing may be out of his hands and thrust into the fate of a merciless world.

He stroked his chin and considered the plan. This Logan seemed to know his stuff. The defenses that the warrior had laid out were

sound in theory, but a lot rode upon the people of New Hope—
people that had never had to fight for their very survival.

Another Gerber baby gave him accusatory looks as he unscrewed
the cap and considered Roy's plan. The coward of a councilman
could be right this time. Perhaps the best decision was to run, to take
what they could and go. They could restart somewhere else. South,
maybe. They had built New Hope from a single old barn and a
desire to be free. They could do it again.

He shook his head and thought that maybe the answer was at the
bottom of another jar of baby food. The door to his office opened
without a sound.

When he lowered the Gerber jar, his daughter stood before him,
her arms crossed, her eyes stern.

"I've only had a couple. It's been an ... interesting day."

"Daddy," she took a full baby food jar from his hands. "I want to
talk about this stranger."

Sarah Wilson looked like her mother, and the resemblance was
uncanny when she was angry with her Daddy. Despite the lectures
he would receive, the scolding he would take, he enjoyed every
minute being told off because of the resemblance. His wife had been
beautiful and his daughter was no different.

"I don't trust him." And, like her mother, she was never indirect.

"Why not?"

"It's all a little too perfect, don't you think?" She cleared off some
of the empties and sat down on his desk.

"I'd hardly call the situation perfect." The mayor realized that he
had never questioned the validity of the stranger's claims. The video
had been proof enough. Hadn't it?

"First of all, that other guy shows up. And he's a moron—
according to Mr. Tinner."

"Sweetheart, call him Roy. It makes my skin crawl when you
show him respect."

"Roy," she said through stern eyes that instructed him not to
interrupt again. "Then this rugged man, a superhero by comparison,
shows up moments later with news of impending doom. He all but
forces us to let him stay. And then we put our safety in his hands."

"I don't see what you're saying, dear."

"It all seems too easy."

He reached for another jar of booze; she moved it out of his reach. "Too easy? I'm exhausted by it. Besides, we asked him to help. He didn't force anyone to do anything."

"I don't trust him."

"You said that already."

"Daddy!"

"Princess, I understand your concern, but these are desperate times. Should these raiders, these bastards come this way ... it's likely that I won't have to live with the consequences. It's you. They'll be done with me and take you to God-knows-where to do God-knows-what. And God knows that I can't let that happen."

Sarah was quiet. She didn't like being dismissed. Scooping the last few baby jars of booze from the desk, she made her way back to the door. It shook the walls of the partitioned office when it slammed behind her.

"I can't lose you, too," the mayor whispered after her. His head sunk into his hands, his fingers tearing at his graying hair. With a broad stroke of his arm, he swept the empty baby jars from his desk.

They clattered as they hit the ground, but none broke. He sighed heavily and pulled a pickle jar from his desk drawer.

# 10

At first he was surprised that he came to at all. Soot covered him. His eyes were caked with the dried ash. Groaning as he rose, he pulled a handkerchief from his rear pocket and brushed the gray crust from his eyes. Once he could see, he realized that he had fallen inches short of the bulletproof safety of the brick wall.

"Your dog is a jerk," she said. Her voice was close.

Pain shot through his head as he turned to face her for the first time.

She sat close, a few feet away; her legs were drawn up in front of her. Chewy sat across from the girl; the hunting rifle was locked in the dog's mouth.

Fuzziness dominated his thoughts as he responded. "Yeah, but she's man's best jerk. Wait, that didn't sound right."

"Pervert."

"That's not what I meant. I was trying to say that ..." He leaned against the wall to clear his head. The brick structure he had sought for protection collapsed under his weight. He fought to maintain his balance. His arms pinwheeled. He thrust his hips with a rhythm that betrayed his dance talents as somewhere between "pathetic" and "high potential for injury."

It was a fierce but brief struggle against gravity; he lost by a slight margin. He stood back up and tried to act as though nothing had happened.

She rolled her eyes.

Take away the dirt, the soot-gray tearstained cheeks, and ashen clothes, and there would be no denying the young woman's beauty. Fierce eyes blazed through the dirt and dust to reveal a sharpness that could see beyond the immediate, the misleading, and drill to the truth in any person.

He sighed and forced a smile that would put her at ease. The pain made it difficult, but he managed. "Can me and my jerk help you?"

"Me? You're the one who's bleeding."

Feeling the top of his head, he discovered a paste of ash and blood beneath his hair. Grinding the mixture between his fingers, he looked at her. "Did you shoot me?"

She huffed and gestured to the dog with the gun in its mouth. "You jumped into the wall, dumb ass."

"Dumb ass? That's hardly fair."

"I told you to stay still."

"So you could shoot me!"

She crossed her arms and pouted.

"Who are you?"

She pouted more.

"Please?"

She went into hyper-pout. He had seen it in children, but he was unaware that an adult was capable.

"Chewy. Give her the gun."

The mastiff growled.

"Give it to her!"

The giant dog obeyed and dropped the gun at the young woman's feet.

The lone survivor of Vita Nova looked at the ash-covered nomad. She cocked her head and half squinted at the man as he sat patting the dust from his jacket and jeans. Her confusion grew as he turned his back to her.

She reached for the gun.

Chewy put her paw on the weapon.

She looked at the dog then back to the nomad. "Erica. My name is Erica."

The nomad nodded and Chewy removed her paw. "It's just a pleasure to meet you, Erica."

Erica picked up the rifle. "Ewww, it's all drooly."

"Erica, meet Chewy."

The large dog woofed at the young woman and kept a wary eye on the gun as she wiped it clean. Erica made no move to arm the rifle.

"Who are you?" she asked.

"You can call me whatever you want. I'm a post—"

"Dick."

"Wait, I wasn't—"

"Whatever I want, Dick."

"That's not what I meant."

Jerry had never been married, but she gave him a look that he recognized as one a wife gave a husband when he had overstepped his bounds at a party. He relented and changed the subject. "What happened here?"

She began to tremble. Her voice came in spurts as she tried to explain while holding back tears. "A truck. A black truck. They crashed through our gates ... it was over in minutes."

"A black truck?"

Erica lost her composure and broke down in complete tears. "Everybody. Everyone is gone. My friends. My little sister. They're all gone."

Running caused his head to ache every time his heel struck the ground, but he rushed to her side. He put a sooty arm around her. She shook.

Chewy worked her head under the crying girl's hand.

Erica threw her arms around the dog and let the tears loose into the dog's brindle fur.

Jerry stood and placed his hands on his hips. Chewy had stolen more than a few things off his plate in the years they had traveled together, but she had never been the first to console a crying woman.

Erica cried long and hard. She tried to speak, but only hysterical gibberish escaped her lips. It was almost fifteen minutes before intelligible words were spoken. "What am I supposed to do now? Where do I go?"

Jerry had been considering the situation since she started crying. Since she had gone on for so long, he had considered many options for her that covered everything from sitting there to discovering a method of time travel. But the most practical was the best solution.

"There's a town a day or so down the road. It seemed nice. I can take you there."

She didn't say anything. She just nodded.

He offered his hand, but she refused. She stood on her own.

The ruins of her home surrounded her. Staying was not an option. Wind blew the ash into the air and stung at her eyes. Without a word she walked toward the red tricycle. Graceful and composed, she bent over and grabbed the handlebars. Setting the toy up on its wheels, she turned and walked silently past the two friends.

He watched her walk away. She was strong. He admired that. She would survive. No mutant, marauder, or black truck would be able to shake this woman now. She had lost everything she had known and everyone she had loved, and she stood tall and immovable. She would be fine.

"Erica. The truck is the other way."

She fell to her knees and began to cry.

# 11

What does one say to someone that just lost their family, friends, neighbors, and town in a raid by savages only a few years after the end of the world? Hallmark never even tried to lessen the blow of post-apocalyptic genocide. Browsing the racks, one would find a large gap in sentiments between "please curb your pet" and "probably not malignant."

Should a card exist, Jerry pictured it featuring a cute kitten in a precarious situation with the headline, "Life isn't purrrrfect." He didn't want to rule out a cute rhyme that expressed the same sentiment, but struggled to imagine a rhyme for "sister was burned alive." If the kitten was the best Hallmark could do, he thought it was best to say nothing.

The trio walked toward the Dairy Queen. Erica trailed behind the nomad and his dog. Only the ground was at risk of being shot by the rifle held loosely in her hands. Her pace was even, but she walked with a stiffness and malaise. Her gaze never left the road ahead. There was no life in her eyes. There was only sorrow and some ash from her burned-up hometown that had settled by the bridge of her nose. Her mother, any mother, would have called it "gunk."

Throwing a regular glance back to the girl, Chewy would

whimper and place her head under Jerry's hand, encouraging the
warrior to say something. There was no misinterpretation of the
dog's intent, but all he could do was scratch the large dog's head.

"She'll be okay, girl. It'll just take time."

Chewy sat down and just stared at him with a cocked head.

"What do you want me to say? 'Buck up, little camper?' 'Walk it
off?' 'Rub some dirt on it?'"

The dog held his stare.

"There wasn't jack in my studies about this. In all the books,
everyone had already lost everyone. There was no consoling. Only
revenge. Only ass kicking."

Chewy barked.

"You say something then."

Chewy barked and ran back to Erica. She tried to put her head
under the girl's hand, but there was no reaction. No petting or
patting. There was just the half-dead steady gait. Chewy walked
beside her and offered an apologetic whine on occasion.

Long known as the Texas stop sign, the Dairy Queen would have
been a more welcome sight if the soft-serve machines were still
functional. Still, as the comfort of the Silver Lining waited behind the
crumbled roadside eatery, it was a relief to see the familiar red and
white sign.

Jerry longed to clean up, but he knew that a gentlemanly post-
apocalyptic nomadic warrior would offer the victim of a massacre
the first shower. Fetching aspirin and peroxide out of the medicine
cabinet and cleaning his wound would keep him occupied until she
was done.

Heat from the summer sun had added sweat to the mixture of
blood and ash in his hair. Each step aggravated the headache that
accompanied the gash in his head. Still, the thought of A/C put a
bounce in his step. The comfort of the Silver Lining was just what he
needed. The trio rounded the corner of the building.

There was nothing there.

"No ... no, no, no!"

Erica awoke from her daze for the first time since leaving Vita
Nova. "What is it, Dick?"

"No, no. Shit!" He ran to the edge of the parking lot and stared across an overgrown field. Parallel trails had been crushed into the overgrowth. "Shit!"

Chewy barked.

Jerry looked at the dog. "Did you lock it?"

The dog barked again.

"You were the last one out."

Chewy lay down and placed her head on her paws. Her sigh blew dust from the asphalt-covered parking lot.

"What's going on?" Erica held the rifle tight against her shoulder. Her eyes, now alert, scanned the fields, the road, and everything in between.

"My coach is gone."

Chewy barked.

"Our. Our coach is gone."

"Your coach?"

"Our truck. Our home."

Peering into the field, he tried to imagine the people who had taken the Silver Lining. He imagined the thieves' excitement when they found the coach open and defenseless. Cursing himself for not arming the booby trap, he stared into the dense grass. Overgrown and empty, the trail led to nothing. There was no indication of how deep the path ran into the wild.

"Did you leave the keys in it?"

"Of course not." He pulled the keys from his pocket. "Someone must have hot-wired it."

"But why would they take it into the field? Why not just drive off with it?"

He shook his head and shrugged. "Are there any settlements in that direction?"

"No. Vita Nova is the only town for miles." Erica answered and then added, "It was the only town for miles."

Chewy began to root at the edge of the field.

"We were always very welcoming. But we hadn't seen anyone for months. Not until the truck."

Darting into the brush, Chewy disappeared in the tall reeds.

Thrashing grass was the sole sign to the dog's location as she followed a scent deeper into the field. Emerging moments later, she grasped something in her teeth. She trotted back to the nomad and dropped it at his feet.

The Texas license plate rattled to the ground with the vanity letters RDWRER facing up at him. It was bent and rent in several places. Jerry lifted it from the ground.

"Why the walls?" he asked, staring at the plate that had hung from the front bumper of the Silver Lining.

"What?"

"Why the walls? If Vita Nova was so welcoming, why did you have fortifications?"

"Animals. There are some aggressive mutations in the area."

"Shit. SSB." He tossed the plate toward her.

She picked up the plate. It was torn, shredded by claws.

"What's SSB?"

"Super Smart Bears aren't really that smart," Logan explained.

"Why do they call them that then?" a child asked.

"Well, they're smarter than your average bear. But super smart? I don't think so. They can't talk. And they still poop in the woods like any other bear."

A chorus of "ewww," "gross," and "he said poop" stirred from the crowd of children that had gathered around him as he prepared for the defense of New Hope.

Strands of steel cable were spread around the warrior as he continued to strip the filaments from a worn winch cable. Fingers bleeding, he pulled at the wisps of metal and laid them out. Several of the children had offered to help and he set them to work pulling the fibers.

"They're smart enough to cause trouble. That's why most towns have walls like New Hope. If they're in your area, they want your food, and if it wasn't for walls like these they would come right in and take it."

One little girl gasped.

"It's okay. These are strong walls. More than strong enough to keep them out. But you don't want to run into one out in the wasteland."

"Why not?" one of the children asked.

"They're strong. Really strong. I've seen one rip the door right off a car."

"Was it your car?" asked another.

"No," Logan laughed. "Not my car. My car is too fast. And I would never go anywhere near a Super Smart Bear."

"But you're strong too."

"You're right, but those bears are mean. I mean really mean."

"Are there Super Smart Bears around here?"

Logan shrugged, "Super Smart Bears are everywhere."

"Why are they so mean?"

"No one knows for sure. But have you kids ever heard of Boris the bicycling bear?"

None of them had, and they all shook their heads.

Logan finished peeling the strands from a cable, laid several of them parallel, and began to cut them to similar lengths.

"Boris was a big brown bear that lived in a circus before the world stopped working."

"And he rode a bicycle?" chimed a boy with glasses that were too large for his face.

"He did. Every night, in front of thousands of people he would ride his bicycle around the ring of the circus. The people would clap and laugh as they watched Boris ride around wearing a little hat and colorful vest. He was a star."

With the strands cut, he made three equal groups and put them back on the ground.

"And every night Boris the Bear would ride his bike proudly around the ring and listen to the children in the crowd clap for him and cheer his name."

He rolled each group of fibers together and began to braid all three, pulling tight each crossover.

"But one night, Boris, while pedaling his bicycle proudly around the ring, rode over a banana peel that one of the clowns had dropped. His wheel slipped out from under him, he fell off the bike, and he landed on his little hat.

"The children in the circus booed. They hissed and threw popcorn at him. Then the parents yelled at their children for throwing popcorn because it was really expensive at the circus.

"All of this was too much for Boris. He stood up and began to roar ferociously at the crowd."

"Was he mad?" a little girl asked and then added, "I'd be mad."

"He was confused. The children had always cheered for him. Now, they were booing him."

"What did Boris do?"

"He didn't do anything. His trainer ran up and began to hit him with a whip."

"That's mean," said the little girl.

"Boris thought so, too. So, the next night he refused to ride. But the show must go on, so the trainer stood in the middle of the ring and cracked the whip at him to make him ride."

"What did he do then?"

"Boris rode his bicycle. And the crowd cheered and the children clapped. But Boris wasn't happy. He remembered the time that they booed because he hit the banana peel and fell off of his bicycle. He was no longer happy, but really, really mad. He didn't like people, or bananas, anymore. And he really hated clowns."

Logan secured the ends of the braided cable with a strip of metal crimped on each end. He picked up a piece of 2 x 4. Attached to the end was a notched leaf spring from an old truck. He looped one end of the cable on a notch.

"When the bombs fell, Boris was exposed to some sort of chemical. This chemical made him super smart. He broke out of his cage, hopped on his bicycle and started riding. Not for the people, but for himself. And Boris rode across the country. He met other bears, girl bears, and they had a lot of bear children."

"Bear children are called cubs," said the kid with glasses.

"Very good," he tousled the youngster's hair, "he had cubs all over the place. But he never stopped riding his bicycle."

With little effort, the warrior bent the leaf spring and hooked the other end of his new cable to the opposite end.

"Eventually, Boris rode for so long that he forgot about the circus and the children and the whip."

"So he wasn't mean anymore?"

"No, he was still mean. Meaner, even."

"Why? If he forgot about the bad people, why was he still mean?" the little boy with the glasses asked.

"Have you ever ridden a bicycle?"

"Yes."

"Have you ever ridden it for a long, long time?"

"Yeah."

"How did it make you feel?"

The child became shy, but answered, "It made my butt hurt." The potty language elicited snickers from the crowd of children.

"So imagine riding a bicycle for a really, really long time. But without any pants."

He drew the cable back and locked it into a trigger system he had fashioned from an old gate latch.

"So, Boris was mean because his butt hurt?"

"That's right. And every one of his kids or cubs was just as smart as Boris and just as mean."

The children were silent. He slipped a bolt onto his bowstring.

"If they're so strong and so smart and so mean, what do you do if you run into one of them?" one of the children asked.

"I'd run and run and get away," another said.

"You can't outrun them, dummy. They ride bikes."

"He's right. You can't outrun them," Logan said.

"So what can you do?"

Logan turned from the crowd and squeezed the gate latch. The energy of the fabricated bowstring unleashed the bolt toward a cinder block wall. The bolt whistled as it soared across the courtyard and drove itself into the block.

For one moment, the kids were silent and then they went wild, cheering and applauding the potential violence offered by the device. They ran over to look at the homemade crossbow.

"Can I try?"

"That's so cool!"

"I want one!"

"I'm asking for one for Christmas!"

"When I grow up I'm going to hunt Super Smart Bears with one of those!"

"NO!" Logan's voice silenced the crowd. There was a harshness to it they had never heard. It grew calmer as he continued.

"Listen to me, kids. Super Smart Bears are dangerous. Don't go near them. Run home and get behind a wall. Only a complete moron, only the stupidest person on Earth, would ever go looking for Super Smart Bears."

"I'm going after them, that's what I'm doing." Jerry stood in the middle of the path left by the stolen motor coach.

"But that's stupid, Dick." Erica had become anxious since seeing the shredded license plate. She gripped the rifle tighter and kept looking to the high grass surrounding the Dairy Queen.

He shrugged off her insult. "We're not going to survive without some form of transportation."

"Then why don't we find something that doesn't have mutant bears in it?"

"They couldn't have gotten far." He walked into the brush. Chewy kept a cautious pace behind him, keeping equal distance between the warrior and the girl.

Erica was terrified of chasing after the bears, but the farther he wandered into the field, the more anxious she got.

She rushed into the field and caught up to the nomad. "I hate you, Dick."

"I know."

Hardened by the fierce summer sun, the ground had provided a quick and firm surface for the coach. But as they moved farther down the path, it became clear that bears were not good drivers. Meandering through the overgrown reeds, the trail often doubled back on itself, causing the trio to retrace their steps several times.

Wide looping turns led him to believe that the bears had not hot-wired the vehicle, but rolled it into the brush while fighting the unresponsive power steering.

The idea that the bears had not yet mastered electrical systems came as a relief, but it worried him that the bears had not thought to place the vehicle in neutral. Stripped gears would ruin his plan of sneaking on board the Silver Lining and driving away really fast, avoiding a confrontation with the intelligent mutations.

With every step down the trail he tried to convince himself that going after the coach was the right thing to do. If the world blowing up had taught humanity anything, it was to not get attached to stuff. Stuff didn't save anyone when the bombs fell, the rivers burned, and the germs spread. Stuff just got in their way. It weighed them down as they evacuated. It possessed some to stay in harm's way.

It wasn't surprising. The majority of the world had pursued the accumulation of stuff: bigger homes, fancier cars, more advanced TVs, smart phones, and more.

They kept smart phones in their pockets and family and friends at arm's length. And when the end came and there was initial chaos and rampant starvation, people learned all too well that you could not rely on stuff. You needed friends. A dead phone provided no companionship, an empty house no comfort. The latest fashions provided no food, but you could always eat a close friend.

Since the commencement of the new world, a stronger emphasis on social circles had formed, not by ones and zeros, but with face-to-face interaction. The accumulation of stuff was not a priority outside of the necessities.

Before the apocalypse, he had less stuff than others, but he had learned the lesson as well as other survivors. He learned to let go of the comforts of the old world. Stuff was just stuff, no matter how cool it was.

Deep down he knew he should leave the motor coach to the bears. He could survive without it. He had before. The home was a luxury, filled with other luxuries that made survival easier.

However, it was also a labor of love. Hours of wiring, tuning, and fabricating had gone into the defenses, the filtration system, and the home theater. His guilt was buried by the reasoning that if an enemy could wipe out an entire town unabated, the few guns the trio had would be of no help should they encounter them on the road to New Hope.

Once Erica had caught up, Chewy moved out in front of the group looking for a trail as if the beaten path wasn't enough. Happy to be helping, her tail wagged furiously as she nosed the trail. Her tail went straight.

Jerry held out his arm and stopped Erica in mid-stride.

Bristling, the mastiff dropped her front shoulders, ready to pounce.

He switched the safety off of the pistol-gripped shotgun. The lack of shoulder stock made it hell on the wrist. He feared having to pull the trigger. However, it was the meanest looking shotgun he had come across and always made for the best impression. Loaded with slugs, it would be effective against the nine-hundred-pound mutants.

Chewy stared down the trail. Her growl grew louder. Creeping forward, her attention was focused on a bend in the trail. Then, her head snapped to the right.

A furry mass burst from the growth and swept across the trail, enfolding Chewy within its mass. The two beasts disappeared into the reeds and weeds of the overgrown field. Vicious barks and ferocious growls from both made Jerry nervous.

The rage of the Super Smart Bears was evident in their roar. It was tremendous and it reverberated through the brush as if amplified. The roar swallowed Chewy's growls and barks.

The warrior rushed into the tall grass, shoving stalks aside with the barrel of the shotgun. "Chewy!"

Large shocks of growth rustled around him as the two creatures wrestled unseen. He began ripping out handfuls of grass in a desperate attempt to find his friend.

"Chewy! Come here!" He stepped left, then right, trying to locate the ever-moving struggle. The thought of losing the motor coach worried him. The thought of losing his best friend terrified him.

With reckless abandon, he chased after each crash and shuddering patch of growth.

Then the roaring stopped. The crashing faded. The grass in front of him rustled.

With trembling arms, he gripped the shotgun tight. Gasping for breath, he tried to see through the reeds. He tried to determine what was shadow and what was animal. Something moved.

A mass of brown fur burst from the bushes and rushed toward him. Despite being a massive dog, there was no mistaking her for a bear. Chewy appeared to be smiling as blood dripped from her muzzle. Her tail whipped back and forth as she trotted, knowing that she had done well.

The grass behind her was still.

"Chewy!" He rushed forward to embrace the dog. She licked at his hands and face. He pushed her away. "Gross, dog. Sit."

Chewy obeyed as he pulled the handkerchief from his pocket and wiped the blood and dog slobber from his face and hands.

"What kind of post-apocalyptic nomadic warrior carries a hanky?" Erica stood behind him, her rifle aimed at the wall of brush.

"The kind that used to be a Boy Scout." He placed the handkerchief back in his pocket. "Besides, you have no idea how much this dog drools. She gets it on the steering wheel and you could be in the ditch in a split second."

She looked around. "What do you think happened?"

"Isn't it obvious? Chewy ate the bear."

She huffed. "Don't you think it's a little stupid to keep going?"

"What do you mean? We've got Chewy." He scratched the dog behind the ears.

"Let me rephrase that. Don't you think you're a little stupid to keep going?"

"To travel without the truck would be suicide."

"And this isn't?"

"To tell you the truth, I'm less worried now than I was before."

"Well, that answers my question. You are stupid."

"Hardly. Odds are in our favor now. Every single time we've run into a Super Smart Bear, everything has been okay."

"That doesn't make any sense."

"Doesn't it?"

"That makes less sense."

"Look, Super Smart Bears are feared for their aggressiveness. I always heard that once provoked they were all but unstoppable. That apparently isn't the case."

"It's still crazy. Surely there's more than one."

"I don't doubt it. Now they know that we're coming. And, if they're so smart, they're waiting right at the end of the trail."

"You're not selling me on this idea."

"They can wait at the end. We've got a new trail to follow." He pulled back the reeds in front of him. Bright crimson marked the path of the fleeing bear.

# 12

Logan had left the children pulling apart strands of cable. He had made a joke about tetanus that they didn't understand, and went to find the town's gadget man.

The mayor had not described him. No one had told him the man's name. Regardless, Logan knew who to look for. Whether he was tall or short, the man would be round and a little grizzled. The man in charge of keeping the town running would have a lame sense of humor and a personality that many tolerated only because he maintained the machinery and invented things that the people needed most: water pumps, steam engines, and more. If not for these vital skills, the gadget man of any post-apocalyptic town would be friendless and, more than likely, left in the wilderness.

Logan found Carl Parker chatting to several men. Each had one foot out of the conversation waiting for the short round man to take a breath so they could excuse themselves. They had been waiting for a while.

Carl was regaling them with a series of jokes about the difference between men and women when Logan interrupted.

"Are you the gadget man?"

Carl turned to Logan and smiled.

The crowd scattered, each tossing a weak excuse over the shoulder as they moved away. The men split. Each went a separate direction as if they were being pursued by an axe murderer or the forces of the undead and were trying to lose their hunters.

"Howdy, stranger. Do you know the difference between men and women?"

Logan did, and the answer was, "Vaginas."

"Well, yeah but that's—"

"Are you the gadget man?"

Carl's round face lit up and he stood a little taller, which wasn't much because he was barely five-foot-five. "Around here they call me the Gadgeteer."

Carl pulled a four-pound sledge from his belt and held it triumphantly above his head. His grease rag rippled like a cape from his back pocket.

"The Gadgeteer. Really?"

"No," Carl sheathed the sledge, dug the oily rag out of his pocket and began to wipe his hands and forehead. Nothing was wiped away; the rag just added grease to his hands and forehead. "I've asked them to. They say the decision is stuck in committee. But if you're asking if I'm the one who keeps this town running, well, yes, that's me. Mechanic, electrician, plumber, engineer, and umpire for the New Hope kickball league."

Pivoting like a Weeble, he turned and began to walk across Town Square. Motioning with the oily rag, his tone changed from one of pride to one that was much more bitchy.

Logan followed.

"Yeah, I'm the gadget man, not that you'd know it if you looked in my shop. I don't have two wrenches to turn together. And the people they send me ..." Carl shook his head. "Everyone is sent in rotation, so just about the time I've got them trained, they leave."

They reached the open hood of a small blue and white pickup. Carl pulled a wrench from his tool belt and buried his head in the engine compartment.

"I tell you, that Murphy is a sonofabitch."

"Which one was Murphy?"

Carl laughed loud and hard at Logan's remark. It was an irritating laugh that sounded like it belonged in the front row of a laugh track. Still, the mechanic was genuine. The round man reached up and slapped Logan on the shoulder with an oil-covered hand.

"No, Murphy the lawyer."

Logan's confusion showed on his face.

"My friend, I'm talking about Murphy's Law that says shit's gonna happen."

Logan nodded. This was the town's gadget man. He took another greasy slap on the shoulder and watched Carl dive back under the hood to tend to the pickup's engine.

Metal clattered, tools clanged, but there was no end to the chatting. Carl continued the conversation with Logan, while simultaneously cursing the engine.

"So, now you know who I am ... sonofabitch ... stranger. And, I know who you are ... little turd. You're the ... mother humper ... man who's gonna save New Hope ... you bastard. The man with the Mustang."

For a moment Logan considered closing the hood and walking away. But he needed this man's help. "I'm going to do my best."

"And I'm guessing ... little beggar ... that you're going to need something from me ... filthy whore."

"I can come back."

Carl's head popped out of the truck's hood, somehow even dirtier. "Why?"

"You seem to be busy."

"No, it's all right. Keep talking. I've just got a nut stuck."

Before Logan could continue, Carl reached out and slapped him again as he began to laugh.

"Sounds like a personal problem! Right?"

Logan could only nod and hope that the mechanic would stick his head back in the truck.

"I know, I know, TMI, TMI, too much information," Carl laughed again and attacked the nut with more vigor. The truck shook as the laughter echoed in the compartment.

"You're right," Logan tried to talk over the laughing, swearing, and clanging. "I need your help reinforcing the gate."

"Well, I only designed it to keep the animals out. We can ... crap ... always weld some more steel on it ... rat bastard. Put a few more inches between us ... that's what she said ... and the bad guys, dammit."

"I had another idea."

"Oh yeah? What's that ... little bitch?"

Logan knocked on the hood. "I hope that was directed at your nuts."

Carl emerged again. "Come again?"

"That comment."

Carl didn't look any brighter when he was confused. He replayed the conversation in his head and it dawned on him, "Oh, no no no, no, no. Yes, I was swearing at my nuts."

Logan shook his head, knowing what to expect.

Carl slapped him on the arm—Logan thought he might be starting to bruise—and laughed louder than before. It took him a moment to catch his breath, and still, he chuckled.

"TMI! TMI! Huh? Ha-ha. What's your idea?"

"I came across an old cement truck, maybe ten miles down the road. It had a hardened load in the back ..."

Carl smiled and was about to speak. Logan hurried on before the mechanic could interrupt.

"A little plating and it would make a solid gate ... if you could get it running."

"When you said hardened load, I was going to say—"

Logan held up his hand. Carl stopped. Logan smiled and said, "If we go right now, I'll even call you Gadgeteer."

Carl smiled, pulled the sledge from his belt and began tapping it in the palm of his hand. "Let's go get her."


Across the plains and down a hill, they followed the trail of blood left behind by the Super Smart Bear to a tree line.

It had made no attempt to cover its tracks as it fled back to its home. The trio dashed through the brush, following snapped reeds and crimson drops.

The nomad held the shotgun high, ready to fire at the first sight of fur. So far, they had encountered no other bears on the trail.

The growth had led to the edge of a forest. He peered into the trees and saw no movement, but he did see his motor coach. The Silver Lining rocked back and forth.

"So, this is where the Teddy Bears have their picnic," he said under his breath and was glad no one had heard him, because right after he said it, he felt stupid.

Chewy growled. Jerry turned quickly to hush the dog. Too quickly. His left foot slid in a patch of mud. Grabbing a tree for support, he caught himself and examined his footing. It wasn't mud.

"Shit." He tried to scrape his boot clean in the grass. "I guess the answer is ... they don't always."

He turned his attention back to the motor coach and its surroundings. He could see no other bears. Their cave must have been deeper into the forest. If the others were there it could work to his advantage.

"What are you going to do, Dick?" She never delivered the nickname as anything but an insult.

"I'm going to watch for a while and when the sun goes down, I'm going to get my home back. Then we'll drive it out of here."

"Won't it be difficult to see?"

"In the dark? Yes, but all the bears will be asleep."

"Aren't bears nocturnal?"

He was silent for a moment. "What? No."

"Are you sure? I think they're nocturnal."

"I never saw a nature documentary of a grizzly night fishing. They aren't nocturnal." It was the end of the discussion. Until it wasn't.

"What about all the dangerous animal shows that played night vision video of bears raiding trash cans and dumpsters?"

"Uh." He had seen those. "That's different."

"How?"

He didn't know. "It just is. Nature documentaries are way more reliable than TBS specials."

She remained silent.

"Look, who do you trust to know more about bears, Marlin Perkins or Vegas's Robert Urich?" he explained.

"I just think it would be best to go down there now instead of when you can't see. You could sneak in. Chances are they're trying to get your food and they're distracted. You'll have them cornered."

"First of all, do you have any idea how stupid that is? Sneak up on bears? Corner bears? Second of all, blood is almost impossible to get out of the upholstery. Theirs or mine. No, thanks. I'll wait for them to get bored and go home."

"Whatever, Dick. It's your precious truck. Besides, I thought you were some great warrior, but I guess you just wear the clothes." She put her back to a tree and crossed her arms.

He sighed, "You know, you're pretty fussy, for a woman in distress."

"Oh, so now it's because I'm a woman. I couldn't possibly know if bears are nocturnal or not, because I'm a girl. Is that it? I couldn't possibly have a good plan, because I'm a woman."

He gritted his teeth, "I don't like having my words turned against me like that."

"Oh, I'm sorry, sir. Was I being disrespectful to your male superiority? Well, forgive me, sir. I forgot my place. I won't say another word. I'll just sit here and look pretty."

She slumped to the ground and turned to look away from him. She did look pretty.

Chewy walked over and put her head in Erica's lap. The dog whimpered, then snorted in Jerry's direction.

"You ... now ... listen ... garhgh!" He dropped the shotgun to his side and drew a .45 automatic from the holster on his hip.

"You just ... you two ..." He raked the slide to chamber a round and placed it back in the holster.

"You two wait here." He grabbed the pistol grip on the shotgun and crept into the forest toward his motor coach and, hopefully, a bit of his dignity—if he could get it back.

Chewy whimpered and looked up at Erica with big brown eyes.

"We girls have to stick together, Chewy. I knew I could count on you."


Every ruffle of a leaf registered as a threat. Acorns dropping from trees were met with a threatening wave of the shotgun barrel.

His senses were acting on overdrive and the closer he got to the motor coach, the more threats he perceived from the surrounding woods.

There was a sudden deafening roar. Wet with rage, the warning echoed throughout the woods. He spun, shotgun at the ready, looking for the creature.

There was nothing. He froze for what seemed like minutes before creeping forward to the motor coach.

Approaching from the rear, his eyes swept the surrounding forest, looking for smart bears, dumb bears, and boogie men in general.

The coach was quiet and still with the exception of the occasional sway from the bears' movements.

It couldn't be just one. One bear, no matter how smart, couldn't roll and steer the coach to a clearing in the woods. There had to be two or more.

If they were in the cabin, it would be a problem. What scared him even more was the possibility that they weren't in the cabin. If he had them cornered he stood a chance, but in the open he would be no match for the superior strength and speed of the hulking beasts.

Another roar overtook the clearing in the woods. It seemed to come from everywhere and nowhere. His imagination placed the giant creatures behind trees, lurking, awaiting a momentary lack of attention before rending him as they had the license plate.

Apart from almost overkilling a squirrel with the shotgun, he reached the rear of the Silver Lining with little incident.

It rocked back and forth on its suspension. The rocking was subtle, but it was enough that he figured it would go unnoticed if he climbed the ladder to the roof and peered in through the skylight. He had to know how many were inside.

He reached the top and slid on his stomach to the rear skylight, which looked into the modified storage space behind the cabin. There were no bears in there. The cargo looked untouched.

Inching forward, the pistol grip of the shotgun never leaving his hand, he made his way to the second skylight and peeked in.

Two massive pelts of brown fur rushed about in the cabin trying to pull open doors and cabinets in a search for food.

The locks he had installed throughout the motor coach were holding their own against the mighty creatures.

A third bear sat on the couch, buckled over, and rocked back and forth. It seemed to be moaning and grasping, its hand between its legs. Chewy's attacker was in obvious pain.

The bears made noises as if they were communicating. It was unintelligible, like a muffled growl, but they seemed to understand one another as they moved about the cabin, occasionally comforting the wounded ursine.

Smiles were hard to come by after the world blew up, yet a grin crossed his face. They were distracted. He had a chance.

He began to move away from the skylight when he heard a scream come from inside. Glancing back in, he saw something that disturbed him. The bear on the couch was grasping and shaking his own head.

The other bear screamed at him.

Surrounding him again was the tremendous roar. This time it was the same he had heard when the mutant animal tackled Chewy into the woods—blood curdling and vicious.

He rolled over, expecting to see the monstrous creature towering above him.

There was nothing there.

He peered into the branches and discovered the source of the roar. There were several of them perched high in the limbs of the trees. Loudspeakers.

"I can't fucking breathe in this anymore."

The nomad turned his attention back to the bears inside.

The one sitting down had removed its head and placed the bear mask aside. He was young, only a child.

One of the bears roared at him.

"I'm not putting it back on. Find something for my hand. That damned dog almost tore my finger off. And it's probably infected."

One of the bears went back to working on a drawer.

The other yelled back at him. His true voice muffled by the bear mask.

"They're not going to follow me. The dog may have bit me, but they were scared. You should have seen that dude. The only reason he didn't pee himself is because he was too scared."

There came a muffled argument.

"Yes. Yes, you can."

Another muffled argument came from the bear.

"You can too be too scared to pee yourself. Now, quit being a jerk and help me."

The bear gave him the finger and went back to searching the coach for food.

Jerry had seen enough. Without a sound, he slid over the edge of the motor coach and lowered himself to the ground. He stepped into the cabin and announced his presence by cocking the shotgun.

"For Super Smart Bears, you're really stupid."

# 13

---

Squinting through one good eye, the major scanned the deserted street. The retail center had not been directly affected by the apocalypse. Looting accounted for the missing windows in the storefronts.

Sporting goods stores and food centers were hit after the electronics stores had been picked clean.

Looters had taken everything. In the seven years since the bombs, no store had escaped the scavengers. People looted jewelry stores hoping there would be value in shiny metal objects. And there had been, for a short while, before hunger overtook greed.

Furniture stores were cleared out for firewood. Auto parts stores were picked clean for fuel and parts to run generators.

Pharmacies were often places of conflict, as their looters were more discriminating. People searching for life-saving medicine became more aggressive fighting over a prescription than they did a media player.

The only stores that had been ignored by the rampant looting were the Blockbusters. No one ever went to Blockbuster.

If there had been anything useful left on the shelves of the strip mall, his scavenging team would have already found it. Trained to be efficient and thorough, it was rare that they missed a useful item.

There was one item, however, that he could not ask his crew to collect.

Personal property was not permitted on the truck. That was the code he enforced with his crew, and drilled into them at every opportunity. Everything was for the good of the whole. The truck would carry nothing that didn't benefit the crew or the nation they served.

It was for this reason that the major often gathered his gear, placed his lieutenant in charge, and strolled off into the wasteland alone.

Had his charge ever been foolish enough to question his orders, he would explain that it was to determine, firsthand, that the scavenging team performed to expectations. He would tell the soldier this after striking him with whatever blunt object was within reach.

The truth was more personal.

He shifted the weight of the rifle across his back. High-caliber and scoped, it was a tool designed for bringing down large game. While the major feared no man, mutations populated most of the wasteland. They had spread in a very short time; it was necessary to be prepared for an encounter.

The major touched the patch that rested across his temple; his first encounter with the creatures had taken his eye. Now it served as a reminder to him and his crew that, despite the unrelenting power of their army, and their truck, shit still happened.

The rifle was not meant for people. Should any man, or overly muscular or hairy woman that resembled a man, happen to interrupt him on his excursion, they would feel the wrath of his knife. Worn at his left side and drawn by his right hand, the weapon was his own design. The draw had been inspired by the samurai. The blade's shape was taken from the Khukuri, the legendary weapon of the feared Ghurka warriors. It curved like a boomerang and yielded fatal striking force. He designed the pommel as a lead skull. Struck upon a temple, the skull would render death, disorientation, or severe headaches.

Unsheathing the wicked blade would usually deter any small group of unfortunate opportunists that hoped to ambush him. If it didn't, the sight of the knife's first victim would cause the rest to scatter.

Large strides carried him past a former hobby store. His team would have scouted there to find casting tools and resin mixtures. The clothing stores would have been searched for leather belts and durable clothes that could be cut and fashioned into uniforms.

A glance through the shattered glass of the sporting goods store window was enough to tell that it was all but empty. Hunting and camping departments would have been cleaned out first. Those arriving too late to grab a rifle or camp axe would have taken the baseball bats.

The golf section was void of bags. Clubs, now tarnished from exposure, littered the floor in the hundreds, providing little in the line of defense or survival use. If the apocalypse proved anything, it was that golf skills were useless skills.

Football and hockey pads would have been secured by the more ambitious who planned to use them in crimes against their fellow man. Those with less sense, but the same intentions, grabbed Under Armour clothing, not knowing that there were very few armor-like qualities to it.

Next door, even dumber people looted the mobile phone store. Those people would spend the better part of a day screaming "hello!" into a dead device and wondering out loud why no one was responding before finally giving up and blaming AT&T, as was the trend when the world blew up.

He continued on to the grocery store. It was a mess. Nothing lined the shelves, but in their haste, the looters had knocked countless boxes and cans to the ground.

His crew would have sifted through the mess, retrieving anything that could be useful. The more days that passed between the apocalypse and the present, the fewer useful items could come from a grocery store.

At this point, the scavenger teams would only enter looking for non-grocery fare. Even food items with a long shelf life had expired years ago. His prize, however, had not.

Shattering glass echoed throughout the store as he kicked the last bit of the window from the frame. He stepped into the lobby and looked around. Even the glass panels in the two ice machines were shattered; looters had no time for doors.

A "wet floor" sign was sitting in front of it. He would never know if it was placed there before everything went to hell, or afterward in an attempt at humor. Either way, he didn't care.

The remnants of stock crunched and squished under his feet as he moved across the front of the store, reading the signs that still hung over the aisles. A couple of them were missing, some hung from only one chain, and one had been re-lettered to read Jack and Shit.

At the end of one row was a coffee bean dispenser. The plastic dispenser was, like everything in the store, empty and shattered, but it was a good clue to what the surrounding aisles had held.

Neither side had a sign. He glanced down the right aisle and guessed that his prize wasn't there. He stepped to the left.

The creature had been quiet. Since losing his eye, the major's hearing had become a more reliable sense. The massive beast had not made a sound as it sniffed the air in the grocery store, hunting for something itself.

The major stepped back out of view. The bear had not spotted him; the creature was too absorbed in its own quest. The gray-haired, one-eyed man drew the rifle from his back and slowly pulled back the bolt.

There was no indication from the beast that it had heard.

The major pulled the rifle to his shoulder and stepped into the aisle. Placing the reticule over the bear's chest, he prepared to fire.

The massive bear sat. It no longer searched the floor and shelves. Its paws held what it had been looking for.

The major spotted the familiar plastic bear in the real bear's paws. The honey container was unopened and unspoiled. He pictured the small plastic bear sitting on his old kitchen table next to her morning tea. The combination of the honey and the Tetley tea would fill the kitchen. The morning tea had always made her happy.

The bear looked up at the man with the gun and cocked its head; its eyes moved from the man to the weapon. It sat still, holding the honey in its grasp.

The honey, the same honey she had used every morning. Anger flashed in the major's eye and he lowered the rifle. "I've come for the honey."

The bear snorted. Its large brown eyes focused on the grizzled man. For a brief moment it stopped pawing at the honey. Then it turned its back to the major and resumed the struggle to remove the plastic cap that held the precious honey in place.

If not for the missing windows at the front of the store, the report from the rifle would have caused a perforated eardrum or permanent hearing loss. Neither the major nor the bear flinched.

The creature turned and examined the major.

Smoke rose from the rifle barrel and drifted up toward the hole he had just shot in the roof.

"I'm talking to you, bear!"

The bear swiped at the litter on the floor and sent the trash twirling into the air. A plastic container slid down the aisle at tremendous speed and slammed to a stop at the major's feet. The major stared down; Mrs. Butterworth stared back.

He picked up the syrup bottle and hurled the old lady at the beast. "I didn't say syrup!"

The bear roared and stood, but it did not charge. Its massive frame towered above the empty shelves that formed the aisles.

"I want that honey!"

The bear looked at the prize in its paw and turned its shoulder to the man, keeping the honey out of view.

"Now."

"Roar!" The bear charged a few feet and stood its full height. Its massive jaws spewed spit and rage. The sound bounced off the steel roof and back down to the empty shelves.

The major drew a finger around the patch. He looked at the small bear in the giant bear's paws. It was his wife's honey.

The rifle clattered across the floor and drew a puzzled look from the monster. The major drew his knife.


The lieutenant was an ambitious man. Before the apocalypse, he had masterfully played the office politics game and risen to the level of director in a Fortune 200 corporation. His rise to power was all but historic in both speed and accomplishment. Promotions came in quick succession while he did almost no work.

Proving himself useful in the post-apocalyptic world, however, had been difficult. Beyond organizing raiding parties and storerooms, there was little that he could do. He had exceptional skill at telling other people what to do, but little ability to do anything himself.

When called upon to act, he had always managed, by design, to arrive a step behind the man in front of him. That man would take bullets and beatings while the lieutenant would take credit.

Not counting the major, he had convinced all of those around him that he was a worthy leader, a fearless killer with a strategic mind. He had worked for years at the deception and with the major's absence he was set to make his move.

No one ever made a move against the old man. Even entering the major's quarters was a stab-able offense. As of this morning, the lieutenant was past the point of no return.

"You wanted to be informed when the major had returned, sir?" The young soldier was a fresh recruit and was obviously nervous.

"Yes." The lieutenant stood, strapped on his gun belt and fixed his collar.

"He's returned, sir."

The lieutenant appreciated the young soldier's weak intelligence. It would make being the new major much easier. "Thank you. You can go now."

The young soldier nodded, relieved to be relieved, and hurried out of the cab, leaving the lieutenant alone in the rig's command center.

He drew his pistol and assured himself that it was loaded. Drawing on the major terrified him and he hoped to avoid it, but he had no idea how the old man would react.

With the pistol armed and holstered, he pulled several items from a box he had discovered in the major's quarters. He laid out the Earl Gray Tetley tea bags on the desk in front of him. This evidence would be enough to accuse the major of code violation. The very code the major strictly enforced.

Standing at ease behind the damning evidence, he waited for his commander. Salutes from outside the truck carried into the cab and he knew the major was close.

Sunlight poured into the rig as he stepped through the door. The major's silhouette seemed larger than normal. The lieutenant blamed his nerves for the impression and raised his hands to shield his eyes from the sun.

"At ease, Dan." His voice seemed raspier than normal.

The lieutenant wanted to protest and explain that he was at ease. His hand was raised against the sun, not to his soon-to-be former officer, but he stammered and left the protest unsaid.

The major shut the door behind him and the cab was engulfed by the sudden darkness. His shadow, even in the dark, looked massive.

Once in the light, the perceived bulk became apparent. Over his shoulders the major carried a large bearskin. No doubt a kill from his most recent excursion.

The animal's teeth were the first things he noticed. The fangs were nine inches long; scarred enamel gave them a jagged look. He stared and had to remind himself to stay calm.

The major shoved the bearskin from his shoulder. Crashing onto the table, the paws unrolled and covered the tea bags the lieutenant had so carefully laid out. One massive claw came to a rest pointed at his waist. The pads on the paw alone were the size of catcher's mitts.

The lieutenant swallowed hard.

"The scavenging crew is to be commended. They missed nothing on their patrol." The major pulled the rifle from his back and placed it on the weapons rack.

"Sir, there is something that we need to discuss." He tried to sound official. Maybe he did. He couldn't be sure if the quaver he felt in his voice had been heard.

The major turned and leaned across the table to look his second-in-command in the eyes.

The lieutenant gasped. The patch was gone.

"Does it look that bad?" the major asked and leaned closer to give the man a better look.

Blood was everywhere. His uniform was a loss, shredded and stained red. Three long tears ran from the center of his face to his ear. Blood trickled from each claw mark bringing fresh crimson to the bloodstained face.

"I had to stitch them up myself. I couldn't find a mirror."

All the lieutenant could do was shake his head. His mouth gaped open. He was horrified.

"That's a yes. It looks that bad." He slid the knife and sheath from his belt and set it on the table. "Have it cleaned and honed. That bastard was a fighter. It took a lot of cuts."

The lieutenant finally found his voice. "Why didn't you shoot it?"

The major had tried to find a deeper meaning to this question himself as he walked back to the rig with the bearskin across his shoulders. Yet, the answer was simple, and it was something that his underling needed to hear.

"It tried to take something of mine, Dan. Something important."

The lieutenant weakened; his blood ran cold and he could feel it spreading through his arms, down his legs to his knees. Buckling wasn't an option, so he placed his hand on the table for support and pretended to examine the pelt.

He stared, through one good eye, at the man in front of him. "It would have been okay if he had just put it back. But he wanted to make something of it."

The lieutenant didn't even consider reaching for his gun. He could only hold the table.

"Please send the medic to my quarters with some thread and a steadier hand than mine. I'll be there in five minutes."

As the major stepped from the table, he added, "That should give you time to put my tea back."

The major left and the lieutenant collapsed at the knees. Heaving for breath, he took a minute to gather himself. It took another minute to gather the courage to move the bearskin and retrieve the Tetley.

## 14

---

"Take off the bear costume."

"It's not a costume. I'm a ferocious bear. Grrrr." The masquerading bear raised his paws. Three six-inch blades extended from each hand. Rust spots marred the surface of the knives, but the honed edge was clean and glinted like silver.

"Take it off."

"GRRRR!"

"Lose it!" Jerry directed the barrel of the shotgun at the bear's temple.

"Fine," the bear sighed and reached up to remove the head of the costume. It twisted slightly but remained attached to the shoulders of the suit. Frustrated, the bear removed the bladed paws and tried again by placing one hand on the snout for leverage; outside, the PA system roared.

"It's not coming off." He turned to the little bear behind him. "Austin? Would you help me here?"

"I'm not Austin, I'm a ferocious bear. Grrrr."

"He's not buying it, Austin. Untie me."

Austin shrugged and dropped his own claws to the ground

before lumbering over to the bigger bear. The two of them struggled for a moment or two to no effect.

"Wait. Okay, bend over," Austin's small voice was weakened further by the bear mask.

The largest bear complied and bent over at the waist. The littlest bear passed his arm over and put the bear in a headlock. Fits of tugging and twisting resulted in the removal of the mask and the smallest bear collapsing on his rear.

Austin, the tiny bear, sat up and removed his own mask.

The three killer bears were three young boys. The oldest couldn't have been more than seventeen years old. Austin was the youngest, no more than thirteen.

"What now, smart guy?" Alex, the oldest, asked.

Jerry leaned forward and tried to dial up the gravel in his voice. "Get out of my house."

Alex nodded to the other two boys. Austin stood up and moved quickly out into the clearing. Trent grumbled and nursed his wounded hand as he skulked from the luxurious coach. Alex waited for the other two to get outside before moving past the man with the shotgun.

Giant insects, rotting corpses, hideous mutants, and other monstrosities of the wasteland were things that he had been prepared to see when he set out across the country several years ago. He was not prepared to see three headless bears, scolded and shuffling out of the Silver Lining. He chuckled at first; it built into a laugh that he tried to hide from the kids.

Regaining his composure, he lowered the barrel of the shotgun and stepped into the clearing.

The bears were huddled together. Alex stood in front of the group, keeping himself between the shotgun and the other two kids.

Laughter still threatened to invade his voice. He fought it back. "How many in your little bear clan?"

The talking bears were quiet.

Jerry moved to the back of the group. There, the smallest bear cowered behind the two bigger boys.

Peering into the eyes of the youngest boy, he growled, "How many rugs am I going to have to make to find out?"

Austin cracked. "It's just us! Okay? We're all alone." His voice quavered but his attempt at a defiant tone emboldened his brothers.

"Leave him alone. He's just a kid." Alex grabbed Austin by the shoulders and pulled him away from the nomad.

"Yeah, you're just being a big dumb asshole." Trent stepped in between the man and the little boy.

"You're all just kids. What's going on here?"

The three looked to each other for assurance that it was okay to speak. Trent seemed to disagree, shaking his head back and forth. Alex only nodded to him and then spoke.

"We've been on our own since the end of the world. Me and my brothers. We were camping out here when it all happened. And we thought we would be okay. My dad was a great hunter; he got us food and water. He told us that it was safer out here than in the cities. But our parents ... they only lasted a year."

"Did they get sick?"

"No." He held up his bear head. "The bears got them."

"The bears were smart," said Trent. "Really smart."

"So you killed the bears?"

"My brothers kept having nightmares." The frustration was evident in Alex's voice. "They couldn't sleep. We stayed up all night just in case they came back. We couldn't go on like that."

"Are they nocturnal?" the nomad asked the boy.

"I don't know. We just waited until winter and found their cave."

"They hibernate just like dumb bears," Austin jumped in.

Trent, the middle child, nursed his hand. Blood began to spill through his fingers. Pain was evident on his face.

Jerry pulled the keys from his pocket and handed them to the youngest kid. "It's Austin, right?"

The thirteen-year-old nodded but didn't come near the keys.

Jerry calmed the grit in his voice, "Inside the glove box is a first aid kit. Get it and take care of your brother."

"Your dog bit me!" Trent yelled as tears filled his eyes. The pain from his hand had become too much.

Jerry fired back. "You attacked a 170-pound dog! What did you think would happen?"

Trent looked at the ground. "I thought I would scare you away if I could take your dog."

"We never had a dog." Austin became excited.

"You don't steal dogs! Or motor homes!"

Austin's head shrank into the safety of his bear costume. Trent took him by the hand and walked them both to the coach to get the first aid kit.

"Please don't yell at him," the oldest said. "He was only seven when the world stopped working. He hasn't been to school since second grade. He doesn't know any better."

Grand theft motor home aside, Jerry admired the kids. They had lasted on their own for years. Many adults had not fared so well. More often than not it wasn't even the post-apocalyptic dangers that did them in. Their inability to get along was often far more fatal. But these three boys, not even teenagers when they became orphans, had succeeded on their own. Even ferocious mutant bears had not offered a challenge to their will to survive.

He called over his shoulder, "Chewy! Erica! It's safe. Come on down. They're not really bears."

Alex stood before him with a confused look on his face. Jerry realized that he still had the barrel pointed at the teenager. He lowered it and spoke, "It's amazing what you boys have done here. To take on Super Smart Bears and not only live, but to wear their pelts ... That's something to be proud of."

"They're not trophies, mister. We wear them to keep warm. To forage for food and supplies. People usually scatter if they see us coming. You were the only one ever dumb enough to follow us."

The nomad shrugged. "You shouldn't have stolen my coach."

"Whatever. We've got to eat. And we're a little sick of living in a cave."

Chewy ran up first and placed herself between her master and the boy in the bear costume. She began to growl.

Alex stepped back.

"It's okay, Chewy. He's okay."

All sense of fierceness left the dog's face. Her growl turned into a large yawn and she wandered off to sniff the area.

Erica arrived a moment later. "Fuck me. They aren't even bears? We've been leaving food outside the town for years to keep them away."

"Thanks for that, by the way," Alex said.

"You little shit."

Jerry began to chuckle.

"What's so funny?"

"You've got a really foul mouth."

"Fuck you, Dick. Can we go now? You've got your precious Winnebago back."

"It's not a Winnebago."

"Whatever. C'mon, Chewy." She slapped her leg lightly. The large dog stopped sniffing the edge of the clearing and joined her new friend at the stairs of the coach.

Jerry turned back to the boy in the bear suit. "You know that Vita Nova was razed to the ground?"

"What's that mean?"

"It means no more food for you and your brothers."

"No, what does razed mean?"

"How far did you make it in school?"

"Eighth grade, but I wasn't very good at it."

"Razed means destroyed by bad people. Ruined. Gone. Burned."

The news didn't faze him. "We'll get by. We always have. Our dad taught us to hunt and survive."

"I'm taking the girl with the potty mouth to a town a few days south. It seemed nice."

"Good for her."

"That's my way of saying you can come, too."

"Oh." He looked around the clearing in the woods. The loudspeakers roared again. They had known no other home for seven years. This stranger was the first person he had spoken to outside of his brothers since his parents died.

"Look, this is your home. If you want to stay, I understand."

The young man stared up at him.

"It's a damn forest, dude. What are we going to miss about that?"

"I just thought ..."

"We sleep in a cave. On rugs made from other bears."

"Okay, but ..."

"These have never been washed." He pulled at the neckline of the bear costume.

"Right."

"You are dumb. Brave, but dumb."

"Fair enough. Why don't you and your brothers get dressed and we'll go?"

"This is dressed. We've outgrown everything else. The good folks of Vita Nova never left clothes in the food pile. And we couldn't very well leave a note."

These kids had put up with a lot. They had grown up without parents in the worst possible world. Still, they had forged a respectable existence. These were good kids.

"Get out!" Erica screamed as a headless bear flew out the door of the coach. The boy tumbled to the ground as Erica came storming to the doorway.

Jerry and Alex ran to help the boy to his feet. Trent had a crude bandage on his hand and tried to push up off the ground with his one good arm. Jerry grasped him by the elbow and lifted him to his feet.

"What's going on here?"

Erica yelled from the doorway, "The little bastard asked to see my boobs."

The nomad looked at Trent. The boy could only blush. Trent shrugged in response to the accusation.

Jerry chuckled again.

"It's not funny." Erica stomped her foot for emphasis.

"Oh, come on, he's a bear. He doesn't know any better."

She stormed back into the coach.

Trent rubbed his head. "My dad used to say it never hurt to ask."

Jerry tried to brush some of the dirt off of the bear suit. "Well, in this case you should have listened to your mother."

"She's really mad," Alex said as he examined the wrap on his brother's hand.

Jerry smiled. "Wait till you see this."

"What?" asked Trent.

"Erica?"

She was red in the face when she appeared back in the doorway. "What?"

"They're coming with us."

Trent lit up. Erica went off—screaming and swearing. Chewy got into the passenger seat and put her head out the window.

"We'll head out in the morning. You and your brothers can get cleaned up in the coach. And you get to sleep indoors tonight."

Alex couldn't suppress a smile. He grabbed the nomad's hand and shook it frantically. "I don't know how to thank you, Dick."

"My name's not Dick."

"But, she keeps calling you ..."

"Jerry, okay, my name is Jerry."

"Thanks, Jerry. I ... I don't know what to say."

"Don't say anything. Just get cleaned up and try to find some clothes that fit. There should be some in the closet in there. We have to make you presentable to the people of New Hope. They're kind of judgey."

# 15

"You're a genius, Logan."

"Please."

"No, really. I'm the guy in this town who can build anything out of anything and I couldn't build a system of flamethrowers."

"I couldn't have done it without you, Carl."

"Where did you figure this out?"

"A delinquent childhood filled with adventure and a touch of arson."

The short man laughed. "I know what you mean. I nearly burned my eyebrows off when I was ten. I'd tell you how, but then I'd have to kill you." Carl slapped the warrior on the shoulder and burst with laughter.

Logan winced, more at the laughter than the slap. "The old WD-40 and a lighter bit, right?"

Carl shook his head. "Insurance fraud. I helped my dad torch our fishing boat."

"Oh, well ..."

"We needed the money."

"I see."

"For a new fishing boat."

"Well, people do what they have to, don't they?"

"I don't know if we had to. Dad was a dentist."

Logan was silent.

"Fun though. And it brought us closer. And, like my dad always said, you gotta have a boat." Carl began to laugh again. It grated on Logan's ears.

A young woman stared at him from across the courtyard. It wasn't the good kind of stare. He could tell she didn't trust him. It was in the way she looked at him through smoldering eyes under a furled brow. It was in her posture, clenched arms crossed, not for warmth but for defense. It was in the way she gave him the finger, perfectly vertical, hyper-extended joints for emphasis.

"Would you excuse me for a moment, Carl?"

"Anything for you, Logan."

"Uh, okay."

Sarah was leaning against his Mustang as if examining the vehicle. She turned away as he approached. Peering into the windows, she pretended that she did not see him approach.

She was beautiful. Jet-black hair and dark skin set off fierce blue eyes and made him wonder if he had ever so noticed a person's pupil.

"Are you checking out the car or me?" he asked.

"Excuse me?"

"I saw you giving me quite the look."

"I don't know what you're talking about."

"I saw you give me the finger."

She shrugged.

"You're still giving it to me."

She retracted the offending digit and clasped her arms tight across her ample chest. "I don't trust you."

"Yeah, I got that."

"You show up out of nowhere, and you've got the whole town eating out of your hands. It's all a little too easy. I don't trust charming strangers."

"You're right not to trust me."

"What?"

"You're right not to trust me," he said again. "I don't trust strangers. I've been burned by too many. And, often, it's the charming ones that mean to do you the most harm."

"You're weird."

"What's your name?"

"Sarah."

"Sarah," he said, letting the name play on his tongue. "You're the mayor's daughter, aren't you?"

She hesitated. "Yes."

"He told me about you. He said you were beautiful."

"And?"

"I figured it was just a father's eyes talking. But he was right."

She blushed.

"Now, don't do that. You don't trust charming strangers, remember?"

She smiled. She tried to hide it and then protested, "I can find you charming and still not trust you."

"That's fair."

"What's your game?"

"What do you mean?"

"You're up to something. And it's not good. I've told my father not to trust you."

"What did he say?"

"He didn't listen. Daddies don't listen the first time. But I'm still working on him." She turned back to the car.

"Do you like the Mustang?"

The body was a vague homage to its former beauty. The ravages of wasteland and driving had marred it with countless dings, divots, and scratches.

Patchwork repairs and armament had left the once polished body a Frankenstein of sheet metal, wire, and bolts.

Contrary to its outward appearance, the mechanics of the car were unmatched. A beast of an engine lurked beneath the hood. A massive blower, the most obvious sign that the heart of the automobile wasn't stock, burst through the hood to swallow air that it would convert into raw horsepower.

The children had flocked to it the moment Logan had stepped into the mayor's office upon arrival. Their fascination had not ebbed in the least.

They had moved closer and closer to the mechanical marvel over the course of the afternoon. Even now they gathered around it. One young boy had even mustered the courage to get into the driver's seat and make revving noises as he moved his hand across the wheel.

"It's not much to look at."

"No. It's not. There aren't a lot of Mi-T-Fines left out there. But she's fast."

She ran her hand along the door, then stopped and stomped her foot. "Trying to get the girl with the car. I thought that ended with the apocalypse."

He laughed. "I don't drive it to get into trouble with the ladies." His face lost all humor. "I drive it to outrun trouble."

She looked back at the car.

"Do you want a ride?"

"No. I mean, I haven't been in a car like this in seven years."

"C'mon, get in. There's something I want to show you that proves you're right."

She scrunched up her nose. "I still don't trust you."

"Exactly. And I would never ask you to." Logan opened the driver's door.

The young boy behind the wheel had been oblivious to the man's presence. When the door opened, he looked up in shock. Logan tousled the lad's hair as the child scrambled out of the seat.

He sat down, leaned across and opened the passenger door.

Sarah smiled and rolled her eyes. Simple chivalry was unexpected. It delighted her to see it. Still, his charms weren't going to work on her and she wanted him to think that. She made sure that she wasn't smiling when she sat down.

# 16

"Just one boob?"

Erica turned away and tried to ignore the boy and his requests.

"Just a little?" Trent indicated with his finger and thumb that when he said a little, he meant a lot.

"For the last time, no! Who taught you your manners?" Erica had had enough of the boys from the woods. Their endless fascination annoyed her. The shower, clean clothes, soft beds, and everything inside the coach delighted and amazed them. Erica appreciated the fact that they had lived in the wilderness for seven years, but the "oohs," "ahhs," and "awesomes" had worn thin well before bedtime.

The oldest one hadn't stopped talking, asking question after question about the world outside the woods. The middle child hadn't stopped staring, mostly at her chest. And the youngest, well, the youngest just sat on the floor quietly petting Chewy.

There had been nothing in the nomad's closet that had fit Austin. So the young boy was forced to wait in his bear costume until they could find something for him to wear. This had upset the boy at first, but now he seemed quite content to hide in the pelt and pet the dog.

The trip back to the road hadn't been too bad since the boys had to help push the Silver Lining back to the Dairy Queen. That effort had given her a little more than an hour of silence as she sat behind the steering wheel, guiding the large vehicle back through the field.

But, after three hours on the road, sitting with the boys in the back, she was ready to jump out the door herself if she couldn't persuade them to go first.

Trent shrugged off the comment about his manners and went back to looking out the window. His eyes had been glued to the road whenever they weren't focused on her chest.

Alex leaned in and said something to his brother that she couldn't hear and turned to her.

"He'll try not to bother you. It's just that you're the first girl we've seen since our mom died."

Erica looked away. His staring had made her uncomfortable, but her lack of empathy embarrassed her even more. The loss of her town, her family, had numbed her to the pain of others. There were few alive in the world that had not suffered loss. These boys may have suffered more than most. Not only had they lost their parents, they had been cut off from the world.

"Why didn't you boys ask for help?"

Alex turned out the window. Sadness crept into his voice. "We did."

"But, I'm sure that ..."

Alex snapped back, "They didn't. They told my dad that they couldn't feed five more."

It was Erica's turn to look away. Ashamed, she wondered who would have turned a family away from Vita Nova. Tears filled her eyes as it dawned on her that had the family been welcome at Vita Nova, the boys would not have lost their parents.

They rode in silence for the next few miles before she could pull herself away from the passing scenery.

Austin, the youngest of the three bears, was looking at her. Even the bear costume was too big for him. He sat on the floor, his knees drawn to his chest. This forced the shoulders of the pelt higher. All she could see were the large brown eyes of the boy.

These eyes didn't shy from her gaze. They held steady, not sure what to make of the woman.

"Do you like dogs?" Erica tried to introduce a calm into her voice that she just didn't feel.

The young boy nodded and looked at Chewy.

"What's your favorite thing about dogs?"

"They're nice, and fun, and don't try to eat you."

Chewy sighed deep as the boy rubbed her chest.

"Did you have a dog? You know, before?"

Austin shook his head.

"Did you have any pets?"

The boy nodded.

"Fish."

Erica felt a sense of accomplishment. The boy had said little since getting on the coach. Trying to make amends for her earlier coldness, she smiled big and asked, "What were their names?"

The boy looked puzzled. "Why would you name a fish?"

Now Erica was puzzled. "I guess so you can talk to it?"

"What are you going to tell a fish?"

The boy had asked a better question than she wanted to admit. "Swim?" was all she could think to say.

The boy looked back at the dog and began to scratch behind her ears. "Yeah, but they already do that."

"I don't know. I guess it's just fun to name your fish."

"You've got a weird way of having fun, lady."

Embarrassment returned, she dropped the conversation and went back to staring out the window.

"Alex! Look!" Trent shot upright and started tapping the window. His older brother turned and followed his gaze.

"It's a McDonald's, Alex!" The grin on his face was caused by unmistakable glee.

Alex nodded and a smile crept across his face. "Look, Austin. Remember McDonald's?"

Austin did not respond; he stroked Chewy's head with long, slow strokes that ended on her back. The dog's tail wagged on occasion, but deep sighs were the more obvious sign of her contentment.

Trent jumped from his seat and made his way to the cab, holding the waistline of his borrowed pants to prevent them from falling. He worked against the rocking of the vehicle and stepped into the cockpit.

"Mister. Hey, dude," he began to shout as he approached the driver's seat. "We've got to pull over."

"What's wrong?" Jerry asked, assuming the worst.

"Nothing, you just gotta pull over."

"Use the toilet in the back."

"I don't wanna pee. I wanna Happy Meal." He thrust his arm across Jerry's vision and pointed at the former fast food building.

Jerry ducked and weaved, trying to see past the youth's arm. The coach responded by diving and weaving across the road.

"Move your arm, kid!"

The swaying of the coach became more violent as Jerry struggled to see the road. Alex and Erica were rocked from the benches. Trent was thrown across the driver's seat. Only Austin and Chewy remained unfazed.

Jerry slammed on the brakes, tossing everyone forward. "What is going on?" He pulled the boy back to his feet and jammed the shifter into park.

Trent ran to the back and burst through the door. Alex was close behind him, pausing only to tell Austin to "c'mon." The youngest boy sat still in his bear suit, petting the dog.

Jerry scrambled after them and ran into the closing door of the coach. He bounced off the door and lost his balance. Grabbing wildly, his hands found the curtains. The rod snapped under his weight. He fell to the floor of the cabin and the curtains settled slowly over his face. Enshrouded in the fabric, he sat up and felt to see if his nose was bleeding. Somehow the impact had not brought forth any blood. He was a little unbalanced when he stood and rushed out the door, and he fought the curtains the entire way.

Austin looked at Erica. "Now that was fun."

Erica smiled back at the boy. "Yes. Yes, it was."

Jerry caught the two boys as they stood in silence in front of the McDonald's. The front of the building was intact, but the entire rear wall was a pile of rubble and rebar. Looking through the windows, they could see through to the barren landscape behind it.

"I'm sorry, boys. You didn't expect it to be open, did you?"

Trent didn't say anything.

Alex answered, "No, but it would have been cool to get one more Happy Meal toy. C'mon, Trent." The oldest boy turned and headed back to the coach.

Trent looked up at the nomad, this man who said he had been all over the country. What had he seen? Had he seen anything at all? "It's really all gone. Isn't it?"

Jerry placed a hand on the boy's shoulder. "A lot has changed. There isn't much left of the world we knew. But there are people out there. Good people. And when good people get together, good things happen. The world may seem lost now, but in a few years things are going to start to change."

He believed this. More than anything, Jerry had faith that mankind could make a better world than the one that mankind had blown up.

"Things are going to be good again, Trent. It may not be now, or five years from now, but soon."

"So, I've got to wait five years for a fucking Happy Meal? Thanks, man. Good pep talk." Trent shook the hand off of his shoulder and walked toward the McDonald's.

Of all the kids, Jerry liked Trent the least. "I don't know what to tell you then, kid. If it'll help, I've got some juice boxes in the fridge."

Trent's eyes lit up. "You've got a fridge in there?"'

"Yes." He had hoped for less whining, but Jerry had seemed to hit the mother lode of consolation prizes.

"No way!" Trent all but left an imprint of himself in the air as he ran back to the Silver Lining. His feet touched, only lightly, on the steps as he flew into the cabin.

By the time Jerry had made it back to the coach, the boys were all taking turns opening and closing the miniature fridge door. Each would pop it open and stick their face into it, exhaling vast breaths, trying to watch a fog form in the air.

Jerry sat back down in the driver's seat. Erica sat next to him, where there were no questions being asked about her boobs. "Wow."

"I know," Jerry pulled the lever into drive. "Just imagine when I tell them I have a TV back there."

"You've got a TV back there?"

"Well, yeah, it's ..."

She wasn't there. She had bounced quickly to the back and located the remote.

## 17
------

Despite its rough appearance, the Mustang rode smoothly over the abandoned roads of post-apocalyptic Texas. The engine was loud and throaty, and as Logan shifted through the gears it was apparent that the drive train had been tenderly maintained.

"Okay, it's fast." Sarah, having abandoned looking stern, grinned broadly as eroded mile markers whizzed by. She had her hand out the window playing with the wind as the pony car muscled its way down the road.

Logan beamed, "I haven't seen anything faster. Only motorcycles have given her a run for her money."

"So why not drive a motorcycle, big bad warrior?"

"A motorcycle doesn't offer much protection."

"Protection from what? As long as you can 'outrun trouble?'" She smiled as she mocked his earlier comment. The exhilarating ride had robbed her of the ability to frown.

"You can't outrun the rain."

"The rain?"

"In some parts, the rain will kill you faster than a mutant. Plenty of the junk from the war is still floating around. The rain brings it down."

"We haven't seen that here."

"It's out there. And when it hits, you've just got to hunker down and ride it out. Sometimes it can last for days."

"I think you'd want something bigger then. Something with some room."

"Space would be great. But having the speed is more important."

"I don't know. There's got to be a few motor homes lying around. That's how I'd like to explore the new world."

"You wouldn't want one."

"Why not?"

"When choosing a wasteland vehicle you want something right in the middle, like my car. It's fast, not nearly as thirsty as a tank, and it's built solid." He punched the roof of the car. A dull thud responded. "That will keep the rain off and the mutants out."

"I think you just like looking cool."

"Well, there's that too." He smiled at her and she smiled back. Not from the rush of the drive but in a direct response to his flirtation.

"Besides," he continued, "a motor home has its drawbacks."

"Like what?"

# 18

---

"What do you mean it's stuck?" Erica shouted out the passenger window.

"I mean it's stuck," he shouted down from the roof. "If we try to go any farther, we're not going to be able to get it out."

"Well, that's just stupid."

He knew he was doing the right thing by taking her and the boys to a safe town. Constant reminders were needed though, and he kept telling himself that it would be wrong to leave her on the side of the road.

"Okay. It's stupid." He dropped to the ground and walked back to the front of the motor coach where the boys had gathered to see what a stuck motor home looked like. Chewy stood with them and seemed to be examining the problem as well.

Austin pulled at the collar of his bear suit to make his voice heard. "Who would build a bridge that a car couldn't go under?"

"Don't be stupid. Of course they built it so cars can go under," Trent snapped at his younger brother.

"It was fine two days ago. The rain washed out the hill." The nomad couldn't tell if it had anything to do with the content of the metal rain, or if it was just general erosion caused by the apocalypse, but mudslides had been commonplace in his wanderings. The sight of entire hillsides that had swallowed neighborhoods, while once a rampant danger on the West Coast, was now a nightmare shared by survivors of the entire country.

"Or, better yet, who would drive a car that couldn't fit under a bridge? I'm looking at you, road warrior." Erica added.

"I said it was the rain."

"Whatever. Your big truck is stuck." Erica laughed at her own comment and withdrew back into the coach.

"Is there another road we could take?" Alex asked.

"There's always another road. But there's no telling what we'd run into. This road is relatively safe. Everything else on the map looked risky." Jerry had consulted the torn atlas page before getting out of the motor home. The truth was, there was no information regarding other paths. This route was the quickest, and the sooner he got back to New Hope, the sooner he could continue on without the constant criticism from Erica.

"It's too bad there's not a way to make the bridge taller," said Trent.

"Or the truck shorter," Austin added.

"That's stupid," his older brother shot back.

"You're stupid!"

"I am not!"

Austin asked. "How is making the truck shorter dumber than making a bridge taller?"

"It just is, okay. You can't make the truck shorter."

"Stop it, both of you." This silenced the bickering brothers. "The little bear is right."

Trent asked, "About the truck being shorter, or me being stupid?"

"Probably both, but certainly about the truck." The nomad walked under the bridge. The rubble had been isolated to the outside of the bridge; under and beyond was clear. There might be enough room.

He went to each tire and let out several pounds of pressure. The Silver Lining settled a few inches lower to the ground. Erica jumped as the balance of the coach shifted for the first time.

"What are you doing?" she screamed from the window.

"We're making the truck shorter," Austin beamed as he answered.

Jerry pocketed the cap from the last tire, and walked back to the coach's door. "You boys stay out here and watch for clearance."

Austin and Trent took a few steps back. Alex crossed in front of the vehicle to watch the other side.

Jerry settled into the cockpit and inched the Silver Lining forward. The ride was mushy and the wheel response was sluggish, but the massive truck pulled itself through the mud.

"Do you really think this will work? Dick." Erica peered up through the windshield as the coach moved forward.

"It's always worked before."

"You think you're so smart, don't you?"

"I'd never say that. I just read a lot."

He listened for warnings from the boys, but they gave only shouts of excitement as the roofline cleared the overpass. Sharp squeals were heard as the luggage rack intermittently met with concrete. The younger boys gasped, but Alex waved him on.

A rough bump signaled that he had cleared the mound of mud and rock. The coach was back on the road.

Alex and his brothers cheered along as the coach rolled through the underpass and emerged on the other side.

Back in the sunlight, Jerry smiled at Erica.

"Okay, so you did it. Now you've got four flat tires, genius."

He stood from his seat and climbed from the Silver Lining. Behind an exterior access panel was an emergency compressor. Ten minutes later the four tires were filled and capped. The boys boarded the coach and he took his seat behind the wheel.

Erica noted his smirk. "You're luckier than you are smart."

"I'll take either one."

"Shut up, Dick."

"I'm so glad I rescued you."

"You didn't rescue anybody, I was ..."

Chewy barked.

"You're in her seat. Chewy rides shotgun."

Erica began to protest but decided to give in to the dog. She was about to step back into the cabin when her face lit up.

"Oh, my God. I just got it. She's your sidekick. Your copilot. You think she's your Chewbacca. You're a nerd."

"No, I'm not. I ..."

"Yes you are, Chewy, Chewbacca," she laughed, "nerd!"

"That's not why I called her Chewy."

"Sure it is. Why else?"

"She chews shit."

Erica laughed. "Whatever."

Chewy barked again.

"Fine, you can have your seat, Chewbacca." She laughed as she left the seat. "Hey, boys, guess what?"

Chewy took her seat; Jerry leaned over and scratched her head. "Good girl."

From the back of the motor coach she tried to explain herself to the three boys. "It's a movie. It's ... oh, what do you know? You're young and stupid."

Then she shouted, "Let's go, Solo."

Jerry whispered to Chewy, "When she's not looking, eat her rifle."

Chewy snorted and put her head out the window.

The Silver Lining's motor purred and the massive vehicle moved on down the road.

## 19

"What do you think of that?"

"Wow." Sarah leapt from the car and stared in amazement. "Where are we?"

"That was Dallas."

The skyline of the once great city spread out before them. Massive buildings and overpasses, once buzzing with life and power, stood desolate and covered with vines. The Trinity River had filled and rushed the levees long ago, fueling the lush vegetation's growth.

There were few elevated areas in Dallas, but Logan had managed to find a hilltop with a view of the city. Erica leapt from the car.

"I've never seen anything so green. It's beautiful." Plant life crawled from the ground and dropped from windowless buildings to weave a veritable rainforest in the middle of the former metropolis.

"It wasn't always green. Before the war, it was gray and brown. Nothing but concrete and dry grass."

"Uh, I remember Dallas. But I haven't seen it since the apocalypse. How did it get this way?"

Logan shrugged. "Who knows what they put in all the bombs? Whatever hit here caused the plants to grow like crazy."

"Can we go down there?"

"No."

"Why not?"

"It's not safe."

"Oh, but I'll be fine. I've got a rough and tough road warrior to keep me safe from the big bad plants. C'mon," she jumped back into the car, "let's get closer."

Logan didn't move. He stood outside his car, staring at the green city.

Sarah stood up. "It's not the plants, is it?"

Logan shook his head.

"What's out there?"

Logan hesitated, "Not all mutants are animals, Sarah. A lot of people died instantly when the bombs hit. But a lot weren't so lucky. There were those that survived, and those that chose to stay behind. They became something else. Something not human."

"Will they hurt you?"

"They'll eat you."

The girl shuddered and asked, "Why did you want to show me this?"

"Like you said, it's beautiful. Charming, even. But you can't trust it. Also, I didn't have any problem taking a drive with a beautiful woman."

She forced a sigh and smiled. He smiled back.

"So, what's your plan now, Romeo? You've got me out here. But I still don't trust you."

"Would you believe I've got a picnic basket in the trunk?"

"You don't," she laughed. "Though maybe you do, because I can't think of a cheesier move."

Logan pulled the keys from the Mustang and moved toward the back of the car. He smiled at her again and reached for the trunk release.

Sparks flew from the trunk of the car as a bullet drove itself through the pony logo. The report sounded a moment later.

Logan dove for the passenger side of the car and tackled Sarah to the ground.

"Stay down!"

Another report cracked and filled the silent wasteland with the echo of the gunshot.

Moving quickly, Logan grabbed Sarah by the arm and tossed her into the car. With one fluid motion, he shut the door and brought his rifle to his shoulder.

He ducked behind the fender as another shot sounded. It went wide and buried itself in the dirt just beyond the Mustang. Spotting movement behind a tree fifty yards out, he opened fire and emptied the assault rifle's magazine into the dirt at the shooter's feet.

The sniper pulled back behind the tree, giving Logan the mere moments he needed.

The warrior stood and slid across the hood of his Mustang. Bouncing off the ground, his feet barely touched earth before he changed direction and leapt behind the rear fender. He opened the door and jumped into the seat.

"Put your seatbelt on!" he yelled as he turned the ignition. His hand free of the key, he reached under his seat and retrieved a Glock. He raked the slide and pulled the t-grip shifter into reverse.

The Mustang spun and turned 180 degrees, tearing up the turf beneath its tires. Sod flew and the engine roared as Logan jammed the transmission into first. The Mustang leapt forward and he pointed it at the shooter.

The car bounced across the field. Shocks built for the street struggled to smooth out the ride, but the passengers inside were tossed farther than their seat belts would allow. Sarah felt the bite of the fabric against her shoulder and groped for the handle to steady herself.

Another shooter emerged farther down the road and fired three rounds. Each missed the Mustang.

Logan stayed focused on the first gunman. He had emerged from behind the tree and was running through a sparsely wooded field. Clad in black, the gunman dodged in and out of the trees, making his way to the road.

Logan swung wide around the edge of the woods. The back tires lost traction and began to slide, but the girl in the passenger seat could tell that, no matter how much it may seem to be, the car was never out of control. The warrior worked the wheel with precision. His feet worked the clutch, gas, and brake without effort as the engine revved and slowed on command.

The Mustang reached the road and entered it sideways down from where the gunman had emerged. The tires screeched as they took hold on the asphalt. Sarah was thrown against the passenger door.

"Why don't you just let him go?" Sarah was excited and terrified. Her fingernails dug into her own hand as it wrapped around the grip above the door.

Logan rolled down his window. "Those aren't scavengers. They're scouts. And if they report back to the truck that I'm here, things will get bad fast."

The gunman burst from the woods and ran hard for a motorcycle that had been hidden away on the side of the road. He jumped on and kicked the engine to life. The whine of the v-twin engine screamed across the open road.

"You said motorcycles are faster than your car."

"Only if he's riding it. Plug your ears."

Logan cranked the wheel of the Mustang and pulled the handle that sat between the seats. The rear wheels locked and broke free of the road and the car began to spin. He let go of the lever and crushed the gas pedal. White smoke filled the air as the pony car pulled up next to the man on the motorcycle, backwards.

Logan thrust the Glock through the window and fired several times. The Glock bounced in his hand as each pull of the trigger cycled another round into the chamber. Empty casings clattered as they fell to the ground.

The smoke hid the gore of a half dozen gunshots, but Sarah saw the gunman shudder with each pull of the trigger and fall to the ground. The running bike collapsed on top of him.

Sarah gasped and pointed down the road. "There's another one."

The Mustang was eager to please the demands of a wide-open

throttle. Sarah felt herself pulled deep into the leather seat as the powerful V-8 drove them forward.

They quickly passed the skid marks they had made near the field and rounded a turn in the road. The second rider pinned the throttle and the cruiser responded. His head start wasn't great, but it could be enough.

"You're not going to catch him."

"We have to. If they expect resistance when they arrive, our plan won't work."

"But you said motorcycles were faster."

"Not always." With the flick of his thumb the warrior exposed a red button at the end of the shifter's t-grip. He jammed the red button and was rewarded with a hiss and a tremendous boost from the engine. Its roar turned to a scream as nitrous flooded the fuel lines.

Sarah couldn't move if she wanted to. The brute force of acceleration kept her pinned to her seat. She felt as though she was about to tear the handle off the frame.

Logan dropped the Glock into his lap and gripped the wheel with both hands, letting go only to shift to the top gear. Every bounce seemed to coax the car into leaving the ground. The tires protested every turn; the rubber chirped with each bounce and wheel correction. The motorcycle grew in the windshield.

The tachometer needle bounced as Logan worked through the six-speed transmission; the speedometer climbed steadily, and the Mustang pulled alongside the Harley.

Logan grabbed the Glock and extended his arm out the window.

The rider was quick. He leaned the bike closer to the car and closed the distance.

Before he could pull the trigger, a leather boot struck Logan's hand. Logan grunted and the Glock rattled to the ground.

He pulled his hand back in pain. He gnashed his teeth.

"Look out!" Sarah screamed. The excitement was gone. There was only horror in her voice now.

The rider had pulled a sawed-off shotgun from the far side of the bike and was drawing a bead on the warrior.

Logan pulled left and brought the shotgun in through the window. With his left arm he locked the rider's wrist. He veered right and dragged the rider from his bike. The bike toppled and flipped, end over end, as a shower of sparks and shattered fiberglass rained down on the road.

The screaming from the helmet was intense.

Logan held the driver to the side of the car as he sped along the road. The rider's feet and knees bounced off of the asphalt as he tried to establish a footing that was impossible. Every scrape against the road left tracts of leather from his gear on the road behind him. It wouldn't be long before the protective gear was eroded away, exposing skin and bone to the road's surface.

Logan straightened the car and began to slow. He pulled the shotgun from the gunman's hand as the car's speed dropped under thirty. Logan slammed on the brakes and let go of the arm.

The rider fell to the ground and rolled to the front wheel. Shredded clothes and bruised knees did little to slow the rider. Rising to hands and knees, he dug his hand into his jacket, reaching for another weapon.

Logan was quicker. He drove his shoulder into the door and crashed it into the rider's helmet.

The shell cracked down the center and forced the rider back to the ground.

Logan jumped from the car and pulled the man to his feet.

"How much time do we have?"

The rider said nothing.

Ripping the visor from the helmet, Logan stared into the frightened eyes and drove his fist into the man's stomach.

Even through the helmet the girl could hear the wind escape the man's lungs. The rider doubled over.

"Where is the truck?"

He couldn't tell whether the rider had been feigning or was desperate. The rider bolted upright with surprising force and drove the helmet into Logan's chin.

He stumbled back on his heels, trying to catch his balance.

The rider dove at the stumbling warrior. Flashes of light bounced off a knife in his right hand.

Sarah screamed.

Now, seemingly unfazed by his fall, the rider moved with quick and polished movements. The silver blade now moved too fast for reflections to catch. He sliced, stabbed, and hacked at Logan as the warrior struggled to regain his footing.

Whistling as it sliced through the air, the blade's tone changed as it caught Logan's leather jacket with various strikes. Every few slashes were followed by a kick intended to keep Logan off balance. They worked.

Logan threw his body in impossible directions to avoid the blade and the boots that came at him. A low slash caused Logan to double over as he pulled his stomach out of the path of the knife. This left his face exposed to the full force of the rider's boot.

He crashed to the ground. The rider's silhouette blocked out the sun, but he could see the blade raised above his head. It was about to plunge into his chest.

Sarah screamed as she tackled the rider to the ground. Clawing and kicking, she stayed on top of him. Padding prevented her attack from doing much good, but it gave Logan time to get to his feet.

The rider grabbed Sarah by the back of the neck and pulled her face into the top of the helmet.

Sarah fell backward against the Mustang.

The rider was up, standing in front of her.

But so was Logan. He put himself between the blade and the girl and stood his ground.

The rider persisted with thrusts and slices, but this time each was blocked and answered with a strike.

The helmet forced Logan to work the body. He focused his blows at the rider's sternum, where the jacket hung open. These strikes, combined with the earlier dragging, tired the rider; his attacks slowed.

The rider turned and ran.

Logan turned to Sarah. Blood ran from her nose. He leaned down and kissed her. "I can't let him get away."

The warrior turned to give chase. The rider wasn't far, but his head still rang from the kick and blood seeped from the stabs. He started to run.

The rider jerked as a gunshot exploded behind Logan. Several more shots rang out and the rider spun around as the slugs tore into him. The helmet cracked in two as a final shot entered through its side.

Logan stared as the figure fell face first to the ground. There was no movement from the rider. He turned back to the girl. She still lay on the ground with her back to the car. In her right hand, she held a revolver. Smoke rose from the barrel.

He walked back to her. "What did you do?"

Sarah looked at the gun in her hands. She let it drop to the road. "It was under the seat."

"I, we needed to talk to him."

"He tried to kill us."

"But we still don't know how far away the truck is."

Sarah stood and placed her arm around him. "But they don't know that we have you. You did it. And we're both safe." She pulled her hand back slowly. It was covered in red.

"Oh, no. You're bleeding."

"It isn't bad."

"We've got to get you home."

"Home?"

"Home."

She helped him back into the Mustang. She spoke softly to him as they drove back to New Hope.

# 20

"What is it, Dick?"

On top of the Silver Lining, Jerry held a powerful pair of binoculars to his eyes. He mused that he had never spent so much time on top of the coach as he had in the last few days. Still, it made the perfect perch.

Even with the hum of the tires on the road and the whining of Erica's voice in the cab, they had all heard the work of the wrecking crew miles down the road. The sound had concerned him enough to stop the coach and climb up for a look.

"Yeah, Dick, what is it?" Austin asked.

"Dude." his older brother, Trent, slapped him on the arm. "His name is not Dick. That's just what she calls him."

"That seems mean." Austin was confused.

"It is," Trent said.

"But, why is she being mean? Isn't he saving her?"

"I don't know why she's being mean."

"Don't keep us in suspense, oh mighty warrior." Erica had climbed to the top of the ladder and watched him watch the distance.

Jerry said nothing she could hear.

"Lady, why are you so mean to him?" Austin shouted up from the base of the ladder. "He's helping us."

"Shut up, Boo Boo." She climbed onto the roof.

"What's Boo Boo?" asked the boy in the bear suit.

Trent just shrugged. "I think it means poop."

"Oh," Austin's feelings were hurt, but he smiled after a moment's thought. "At least she didn't call me dick."

Trent nodded and watched Erica disappear over the top of the Silver Lining.

When she reached his side, Jerry was no longer looking through the binoculars, but staring off into the distance, deep in thought.

"What's the holdup?" She followed his gaze. It was hard to make out what was happening.

He handed her the binoculars.

She placed them to her eyes. Her face went white and she began to stammer. "Oh, my God. Oh, God."

"It's them, isn't it?" he asked.

She sat down, hard, on the roof of the coach. The binoculars fell from her hand. She nodded, her face a twisted expression of hate, anger, and fear. Tears filled her eyes, but they refused to fall.

Squeezing her hand gently, he sat down next to her. He picked up the binoculars and peered at the rig in the distance.

He had seen the armed guards surrounding the perimeter of the truck. This was not uncommon. Everyone on the road was armed. It could have been a caravan. Trade had started to resurface a couple of years ago. Anyone could believe that a guarded rig was nothing more than a group of honest traders.

There was constant activity as the wrecking crew cleared the road. Looking more closely he noted not only the scene, but also the people surrounding the rig.

One man leaned against the truck, a cigarette burning between his lips. Jerry had used the apocalypse as an excuse to give up the habit. Having figured that tobacco would be impossible to come by after the world blew up, he was surprised that it was one of first industries to bounce back. Originally scrounged and repacked from pre-apocalyptic smokes, the process had evolved to newly sown tobacco plants.

At first glance, the smoker appeared to be on break. Looking back at him now, knowing the true nature of the rig, he noticed that the man was bound.

A man with white hair and a red face stepped out of the rig and turned to survey the progress of the road crew. He yelled and pointed instructions, then turned and walked to the bound man. The smoker tried to stand at attention as best he could with his hands fastened behind him.

The white-haired man struck him across the face. The cigarette flew from his lips along with what Jerry could only guess were teeth and a spray of blood.

He recovered only to be struck again. The white-haired man yelled. Jerry could not hear what was said over the sounds of the road crew.

After several strikes, the bound man collapsed. His face was a mess.

The white-haired man yelled to two of the guards. They responded by picking the man up off the ground. Supporting him by the shoulders, the guards held the bound man as he slumped. Slight movements from his head were the only indications that he was still conscious.

The white-haired man pulled something from his belt.

There was a flash of light and blood began to spurt from the bound man's throat. The white-haired executioner walked away as the guards pulled the body to a wrecked sedan. They placed the body in the trunk and rolled the sedan down the embankment. "We can't, we can't, we can't ... please." Erica had pulled her knees to her chest and pleaded through tears that had finally begun to fall.

He dropped to his knee and held her. "We'll go around."

"No. Let's go back. Somewhere else."

"Erica." His voice was soft, but strong. "We can't. That thing is headed to New Hope. We have to warn them."

She sobbed and shook her head frantically.

"We can't let what happened to you happen to them."

She controlled her sobbing. "They can't be stopped. Don't you see? We tried."

"But I'll be there to help."

She tried to laugh at him, to mock him, but everything came out as sobs. "You? What can you do?"

"Me? I'm a big bad road warrior, remember?" She saw no humor in his mocking.

"Erica," he spoke with a confidence she needed to hear. "This is what I do." It was not a confidence he possessed.

"Bullshit. That's what the other guy said."

"What other guy?"

"The 'post-apocalyptic nomadic warrior' that promised he'd help us. He had a plan, too. It failed. And he's dead now. Just like everyone I ever knew."

He wanted to hang his head. Instead, he looked her in the eye. "Erica. You will be safe with me. I'm different."

"That's what he said. And he was way better than you."

"Erica, I'm ashamed to say, but the world is full of frauds claiming to do what I do. They look the part. They promise to help. Then they take advantage of people. Good people like your family and friends. Chances are he snuck off as soon as the truck showed up."

"No, I saw him. He was dragged into the truck. He screamed louder than the others. They must have tortured him. He was real and he couldn't help. No one could. They walked right through the defenses and destroyed everything."

He held her tighter as she began to sob again. Was this her? The real Erica? He felt as if this was the girl worth saving, not the one who lashed out in self-defense. She was vulnerable and hurt. How could he put her in harm's way? And the boys? They didn't deserve to be pulled from a basic, but safe, existence only to be placed in a town that was in the crosshairs of merciless killers.

Jerry thought of Logan. He didn't like the man, but at least New

Hope stood a chance if he was still there. Maybe they had an even better chance with him than if he was aiding the people.

He placed his hand on Erica's cheek and guided her gaze to meet his own. "Erica, we can go somewhere else. We can. The town is a ways off the road and there's a good chance help is already there."

She looked at him, smiled and sputtered through the tears. She put her hand on his.

"We'll turn around," he said. "We'll go somewhere else."

She smiled and nodded. He helped her stand and walked her to the ladder. She took each step with caution; the focus helped her to stop shaking. Looking back up at him, she smiled, "You're right, you are different than Logan."

He had matched her smile, but it vanished quickly.

"Logan?"

"That was his name."

"Get in the coach. We're going to New Hope."

He expected anger to return, but it was fear in her eyes.

"But, you just said ..."

"Erica, Logan is alive. The people of that town are going to die if we don't help."

She was silent as the truth of the events at Vita Nova sunk in.

"Don't you see?" Jerry asked. "He let them in."

She grabbed his wrists and squeezed. She shook him as she began to swear and curse Logan. The violent reaction threatened to pull him from the roof.

"That bastard!"

"Erica, get down."

"I'm going to kill him!"

"You're going to make us both fall."

She stopped shaking his arms but did not relax her grip.

The scuffle drew the boys back to the base of the ladder.

"Is she okay?" Trent yelled up.

"Alex, Trent, help her down and take her inside. Calm her down. Get her a drink. Don't let her have a gun."

"Is she that mad at you?" Alex asked.

"Just do it."

Alex took a step on the ladder and helped pull Erica to the ground. The boys tried to calm her as she swore at each of them.

Jerry turned to study the rig through the binoculars. He scanned the behemoth for weaknesses. He saw a man with white hair looking back.

# 21

---

"It doesn't look too serious. The ointment should stave off infection," said the town doctor as she finished bandaging Logan's knife wound. "I'm not sure how to treat that, though," she added, pointing to Sarah's grasp of Logan's hand.

Sarah blushed, but did not let go of the warrior's hand.

The doctor smiled and left the two of them alone.

Logan smiled at Sarah. She smiled back and leaned in close; her lips parted.

The door to the clinic flew open and struck the wall behind it.

"Sarah! Princess! Are you all right?"

Sarah dropped Logan's hand and hugged her father. "I'm fine, Daddy. Logan protected me."

"What happened out there?"

Logan pulled his shirt over his bandaged torso. "We ran into a couple of the major's men."

"But we stopped them before they could get away. They're not going to be able to tell him anything."

"But the major will be suspicious when they don't report back." Logan stood with visible pain.

Sarah put her hand on his shoulder to steady him. The mayor

noticed the tenderness. He could see what was happening between the two. He approved. "How much time do we have?"

"Not much. We'll have to work faster."

"I'll let the town know. Just tell us what you need and we'll make it happen."

The mayor turned to leave, but stopped. "And, Logan. Thank you. You're a good man." He smiled at his daughter and left.

Sarah smiled at Logan and put her hand back in his. "I think Daddy approves."

Logan smiled.

"How hurt are you? Exactly?" Sarah leaned in and kissed him. He kissed back.

# 22

"What are you going to do?"

He shoved past her and hit the home theater switch. A bracket lowered his arsenal. He moved frantically.

"I may be able to stop them here." He grabbed the largest rifle from the rack and climbed back onto the roof. Red tape marked an ammo magazine as tracer rounds; he slapped the box into the Barrett .50 caliber rifle and propped it up on the bipod.

Peering through the scope, he saw the heightened activity at the rig. The white-haired man barked orders; his men responded.

Striking a fuel tank with a tracer round should cause a critical explosion. The distance was extreme and he questioned whether the .50 caliber round would even penetrate the armor they had placed around it. Plus, the Silver Lining was shaking.

He slapped the roof. "Be still in there!"

"She won't stop jumping," was the response.

"Or swearing," was the other.

"Erica! Please sit down. I'm trying to shoot the bastards."

The rustling stopped and the coach steadied itself.

Scanning the rest of the truck, he searched for another target. The scope crossed the trailer mounted to the outside rear of the rig. Its plating wasn't as thick. The walls weren't even solid. They were grated, like a livestock hauler.

With a whine, like that of a camera flash charging, the thermal scope came alive and displayed the activity at the rig. Men were replaced with splotches of color. They were scattered everywhere. He pointed the scope toward the rear trailer.

Body heat signatures filled the crosshairs. The rear trailer was filled with a mass of people. The density of the heat signatures lit the entire field of the scope.

The murdered people of Vita Nova weren't dead. They were crammed into the livestock trailer.

He heard the crack of the fiberglass next to him before the crack of the rifle. A second bullet struck even closer.

They had set up their own snipers.

He fired several rounds quickly to force their heads down. He found the tires next. Striking the fuel tank would kill the prisoners. If he couldn't stop them, he could slow them down.

With each pull of the trigger, a tire erupted. He fired five times and each trailer sank as the air drained from the wheels.

The bullets came at him faster as the entire squad opened up. He scurried backwards and to the side of the roof, trying to get out of their line of sight. He looked through the scope one more time just in time to see the gate on the rear left trailer drop. Several motorcycles burst from the trailer. The riders were armed and they were moving fast.

He dropped the rifle through the skylight and followed it into the coach. Barking orders at the passengers, he forced his way to the cockpit and pulled the coach into gear.

"What's going on?" Alex ran to the passenger seat. Chewy was trying to console Erica.

"They're on their way. We've got to hurry."

"The truck is coming?"

"Worse. They've got bikes."

"So? What about the Silver Lining?"

"Motorcycles are fast. Coaches aren't. Plus, it takes a long time to do a three-point turn on a post-apocalyptic highway."

It took more than a minute to turn the Silver Lining and get it up to speed. It took slightly longer for the bikes to arrive.

"Everybody get down!"

The brothers and Erica dropped to the floor. Chewy huddled with them.

Bullets tore through the thin skin of the coach. Cans of food in the pantry exploded. Equipment and supplies fell from the walls.

Jerry swerved left and right as he tried to knock the riders from their bikes. The riders were agile and easily dodged the lumbering coach.

"Erica, take the wheel."

Huddled on the floor with her hands above her head, she hesitated.

He pounded his door. "Erica. It's bulletproof. You'll be fine."

She crawled to his side and they switched places. Her arms shook as she grasped the wheel. He put his hand on her shoulder and leaned in close.

"Just keep it on the road and don't let off the gas."

She nodded and gripped the wheel tighter.

Jerry dove to the floor of the cabin, lifted a panel in the floor and slid into the storage area.

Four bikes had surrounded the coach, each armed with a submachine gun. Pulling alongside the door of the coach, a rider on the left sighted Erica behind the wheel. A shot through the shattered window of the cabin door would end the chase immediately. He raised the barrel of the weapon and prepared to fire.

The lower panel on the motor coach flew open and struck the motorcycle. Letting the gun drop to his side, the rider grabbed the handlebar with his left hand and struggled to maintain his balance. The bike wobbled for a few hundred feet and steadied. He grabbed for the weapon again. Then he saw the man inside the storage compartment. The shotgun blast lifted the rider from his bike and dropped him on the concrete.

Jerry fired at the second bike.

The rider slowed and pulled up behind the coach.

Jerry slammed the outer door shut and climbed back into the

cabin. He slid into another hole in the floor. Unlike the first hatch, this compartment was full of gear, and it was difficult to maneuver around the boxes. He reached the door and kicked open the panel on the far side of the coach.

The rider saw the panel begin to open and kicked back. The door swung shut and knocked the shotgun from Jerry's hand to the road below.

Rearing back from the pain, he fell back into a box that simply said "Chewy" on it. Contents spilled everywhere, adding to the clutter in the compartment.

Hissing, the hydraulics on the compartment door raised the hatch open.

Kicking the panel had caused the rider to struggle for his balance. He regained it as the panel opened. He drew his weapon and waited for his shot.

Chewy's old leash was within reach. On the end was a pronged training lead. It was huge. It had to be to fit around the large dog's neck. It was also heavy.

The rider had to bring his left hand across the bike to fire. Jerry whipped the weighted leash to force him off balance while trying to catch the training lead on some part of the bike.

The rider leaned away from the coach to escape the grasp of the leash.

Again, Jerry tried to hook the leash on the handlebars or the rider.

Putting himself out of reach of the makeshift flail, the rider pulled the weapon across his chest.


Out of desperation, Jerry threw the collar ahead of the bike. The lead caught in the spokes, the training collar wedged into the fork. Sparks flew and spokes snapped as the wheel ate itself. The bike collapsed and the fork drove itself into the road.

The sudden deceleration threw the rider over the handlebars. He plowed face first into the highway. The bike followed over him a moment later.

Jerry closed the panel, crawled back into the cabin and scrambled to the cab. He struck a switch on the dash that didn't look as if it belonged there.

"Brake!"

"What?" Only the leather wrapping of the steering wheel softened Erica's grip.

"Brake!"

She stomped on the brake. The coach lurched forward on its frame. The boys in the back grasped for something to hold onto as they slid forward on the floor.

Jerry was thrown into the dash. Chewy, curled beneath the dash, whimpered as her mass shifted.

There was a thud from behind the coach. A rider shot past them on the right.

"Now, go!"

She mashed the gas. "What was that switch?"

"It turns off the brake lights."

The final rider slammed on his own brakes and turned to race back to the coach. He drew his gun.

"Head straight for him."

"He's not going to let me hit him."

"You don't need to." Jerry hit a second switch. There was a whirring deep inside the hood of the Silver Lining. Slowly, a steel plate rose to cover the front of the driver's windshield.

The rider began to fire. Erica ducked. The coach began to veer.

Jerry grabbed the wheel as bullets bounced off the plate. The passenger side windshield shattered. Jerry peered through a slit in the steel plate and pulled a cable with his right hand.

The Silver Lining's grill dropped and revealed a solid line of barrels that stretched across the front of the motor home.

The rider saw the threat and tried to swerve.

Jerry yanked a grouping of cables that ran across the triggers of fifty-two shotguns mounted under the hood of his post-apocalyptic motor home.

The rider didn't explode, but disappeared into a misty cloud of blood. He caught the blast full on and flew backward off his bike.

The bike continued off to the side of the road and bounced harmlessly down the hill.

"Slow down."

Her foot was glued to the floor.

"Slow down, Erica."

This time she listened.

"Is everyone okay?"

"What was that?" The boys were bruised from the bumpy ride, but otherwise unharmed.

"Fifty-two shotguns all fired at once. I put them there for barricades or zombies. But it seems to work for this too."

He hit the switch again and the armor plate retreated back under the hood.

The boys looked at him in awe. Erica stared at him.

"Take this exit. We're going to have to cut through Dallas."

She responded slowly, but took the exit. The onramp was, for the most part, intact. She navigated it carefully and they merged onto the Interstate highway that would take them into the jungle city of Dallas.

# 23

---

The wheel wobbled. Bent out of alignment, it shook the rider who struggled to control the bike. He had one hand on the throttle and the other cradled across his chest; a bone protruded below the elbow.

Two men rushed to steady the bike as the rider carefully pulled a tender leg over the frame. Limping, he approached his commander.

Pacing the length of the trailer, the major surveyed the flattened tire and grumbled as he walked from one flat to another.

"What do you have to report?" he wheezed as he knelt to inspect the bullet hole. The phosphorus rounds had not only torn through the rubber, but melted it as well.

"They got away, sir. The others are dead."

The major didn't react. He continued to study the tires. Placing a finger through the hole, he found that the tire was still smoking. "They shot my tires."

"I'm sorry, sir."

The major stood and turned to the rider.

The battered soldier flinched. The major had always been gruesome and intimidating. Now he stared, patch-less, into the eyes of the fallen rider.

"Is something wrong?"

"No, no, sir." The empty socket was filled with scar tissue deep inside the cavity. The healing wounds across his face puffed around the stitches. The rider backed away. The major's pale blue eye didn't waver.

"The patch was aggravating the stitches. Hurt like a sonofabitch. It doesn't bother you, does it?"

"No, sir."

"Now," the major stepped forward and took the rider by his broken arm, "let's talk about how they got away." The major dragged the rider down the length of the trailer.

The limping caused him to lose a step to the major. The major responded by pulling harder on the arm.

"Tell me what happened."

The rider bit back screams of pain. "The, the Winnebago was armored and there were guns everywhere."

The pair stopped in front of the prison car. The dirty masses inside peered out through the slats of the former livestock hauler.

"I cannot allow failure in my command." He twisted the rider's arm at the wrist.

The soldier screamed ferociously and dropped to his knees. Twisting his body, he attempted to move with the major to lessen the pain.

"I gave you shelter, food, purpose, and you reward me with failure!"

Crewmembers stopped their tasks and turned their attention to watch the reprimand.

"You're weak." The major tugged on the arm again, exposing more bone. "My command is no place for the weak. This world is no place for the weak. The weak will only suffer. Only the strong will prosper."

He released the soldier's arm and shoved him back against the truck. There he leaned, doubled over, cradling his mangled limb.

"Stand up, soldier! Stand at attention when you stand before me."

The soldier grit his teeth and stood, painful as it was, with his arms at his side.

"Be strong."

The soldier winced.

"Chin up!"

The soldier buried his pain and complied by raising his chin and standing at complete attention.

"There you go," said the major.

With one fluid movement, the major drew his knife and sliced open the soldier's trachea.

Blood erupted from the slashed jugular and gurgling screams rushed from the soldier's lungs as they expelled their final breath. He fell dead at the major's feet.

The prisoners gasped at the sight.

He wiped the blood from the knife on a rag and called to one of the guards. "Send a group to retrieve their equipment."

"And the bodies, sir?"

"Let the wasteland have them."

# 24

---

"I would like to take this opportunity to apologize for my behavior when you first arrived." Roy Tinner shifted from foot to foot. He spoke without hesitation as if he had practiced the spontaneous apology in a mirror. Which he had.

"Don't mention it, sir." Logan instructed the townspeople as they strung barbed wire across the top of the walls of New Hope. Sarah worked next to him. Her smile could light the town.

"You have shown through your actions to be an honorable and capable—"

"Really." Logan placed his hand on the councilman's shoulder. "You were looking out for your town's best interests. That is what these people elected you to do. And you did it well."

Tinner wasn't used to apologizing and even less accustomed to his apology being refused.

"I ... I have to be sus—"

"Yes, you have to be suspicious. There's no shortage of con men out there."

"Yes. Like the charlatan that showed up before you."

Charlatan? This guy was trying too hard, thought Logan. "You mean Jerry?"

"Yes. A con man if I've ever seen one."

Logan laughed. "Jerry is no con man. Delusional maybe. But he's no con man. He's a harmless bookworm."

The puzzled look on the councilman's face led Logan to explain.

"Jerry was a librarian. He was stacking books in a storage room when the bombs hit. Lucky for him, the storage was in an old bomb shelter. He rode out the aftermath with tinned meat and seventy-year-old Cokes."

Logan turned to instruct a woman on how to fasten the wire to the support rods.

"And there he stayed. A time lock on the door held him prisoner for a year. So what did he do?"

The councilman shook his head.

"He read. And read and read. He must have read every book in the place. The books made him smart. Too smart for his own good. When the door finally opened, he was convinced that he could help people."

"That kind of knowledge would be helpful."

Logan looked at the ground and his voice became distant. "They say that a little bit of knowledge can be a dangerous thing. And they, whoever they were, are right."

"How do you know all this?"

"Jerry and I were partners out west. I thought the same as you. This guy was so smart. We could make a difference anywhere. And for a while we did. We traveled from town to town. He taught the folks how to purify water, how to build generators ... that kind of thing. We were making a difference.

"But then there was Eternal Hope. A small town in Colorado. They had a different kind of problem. One that couldn't be fixed with wells or crop rotations."

Logan looked off into the distance in the direction that he assumed to be west.

"Jerry convinced me and the town that he could defend them from a gang of ruthless bandits. He prepared defenses that he claimed were based on sound military tactics."

"They didn't work?"

"They came right in the front gate and we were overwhelmed. Jerry disappeared. I did what I could. A few of us got away. No one else survived."

Roy turned red; the reverence disappeared. "We should have strung him up!"

"No. I don't know how a man can live with that kind of failure. But it can't be easy. The screams are his burden to carry. That blood is on his hands."

"It's dangerous that he offers to help people."

"From what I hear he doesn't offer protection anymore. He'll offer to run for supplies, solve various problems, find missing persons. He can't offer protection. How could he? How could anyone after that?"

Logan pulled on the taut wire. "Good job, everyone."

"You're a good man, Logan. Thank you for saving Sarah. And for helping us protect New Hope."

Logan nodded without a word. The painful memories were written on his face.

The councilman, his apology offered and thanks delivered, turned and walked back to the town hall barn. There was a list in the cabinet that named Personas Non Grata in the town. He had a name to add.

Sarah turned to Logan. "You said people don't come out of Dallas."

"What I know about Dallas, I know from Jerry."

"What's in Dallas?"

"The bombs grew more than a jungle there."

"How did he get out?"

"Luck."

# 25

Dallas had always sweltered. Summer heat mixed with the reflective properties of concrete and drove temperatures to miserable degrees. Even at night, the lack of sun did little to dissipate the heat.

Since the world blew up, the concrete jungle of Big D had been consumed by an actual jungle and added humidity to the already uncomfortable atmosphere. Agent-filled warheads had mixed in unpredictable ways. The resulting compound had caused what little vegetation there was in the Metroplex to mutate and grow at accelerated rates.

Elevated roads had remained relatively clear of the growth. The Silver Lining bounced on the occasional vine but made its way over the surface with a lumbering ease.

Moving up 35 into the city, across Woodall Rodgers and down 45 would keep their path well above the undergrowth. Jerry quietly prayed that the trip would be uneventful, but his eyes darted around constantly as he peered through the shattered windows of the cab.

Erica watched him grow less and less comfortable the farther they moved up 35.

"What's wrong?"

"Nothing. Where's your rifle?"

"It's in the back."

"Get it, would you?"

She stepped into the rear of the home, picked up her rifle and gave the three boys a look that spread her panic to them. She returned to the cabin.

"Here it is."

"Keep it close. And get in the back."

"What's out there? Why are you so nervous?"

"I'm not."

"You can hardly sit still."

"Just get in the back. And send Alex up here."

She made no argument as she moved into the cabin and told the oldest boy to step up front.

He hesitated and looked to his siblings. They, too, had picked up on Jerry's nervous actions. Alex clutched a beat-up hunting rifle for comfort, not defense. Austin had put his bear head back on and gripped Chewy tight around the neck. Trent could hear him weeping.

Alex buried his own nerves and stood. He looked Trent in the eye, patted Austin on the bear head, and moved to the front.

"Yes, sir?"

"Alex, I need you to ride shotgun."

"Yes, sir." The teenager sat in the passenger seat.

"Alex."

"Yes, sir?"

"Grab a shotgun."

"Yes, sir."

The coach swayed as he steered around rubble in the road. Alex was tossed back and forth as he struggled to get to the gun rack. He pulled a semiautomatic 12 gauge from the former TV mount and climbed back into the passenger seat.

Little traffic clogged the highways. Dallas had been one of the few cities to receive an evacuation notice during the apocalypse. Almost everyone complied. The joke in the wasteland was that everyone in the city had been waiting for a reason to get out of Dallas.

"Just keep it pointed through that hole in the window. And shoot at anything that moves."

"What if it's a person?"

"Especially if it's a person."

Alex's grip on the gun caused it to tremble. The clattering of the weapon's action drew Jerry's attention. He saw the fear in Alex's eyes. He wondered if his looked the same.

"It'll be okay, kid. We shouldn't have a problem with the highways."

"Look out!"

Jerry turned back to the road and slammed on the brakes. Ahead, the road dipped to pass beneath the deck park that had been built across the highway shortly before the world blew up.

It had collapsed.

"Dammit."

"What do we do now?"

There was an exit on his right that led downtown. Chest heaving, he struggled to calm his breathing. Fear soured his stomach. His arms didn't want to respond.

Down those roads were the memories of his rebirth into the ravaged world. Terrifying memories.

A breeze blew the rank stench of the jungle's rotting undergrowth through the busted windscreen. He inhaled it deeply, refusing to choke on it. It smelled like him—Jerry's first nightmare in the new world. His raspy voice echoed in Jerry's head with dull thuds that repeated in a constant rhythm.

Chewy whimpered. She remembered the smell.

"What is it, Jerry?" Erica's voice shook.

The sound of her not calling him a dick stopped his breath short. A moment later his breathing returned to normal. The shaking stopped.

"It's nothing. Everyone hold tight. We're going to make this quick."

Jerry cranked the wheel and pointed the massive vehicle into the overgrown streets of downtown Dallas.

## 26

Beneath the pileup was a layer of clear blacktop that had been protected from the ravages of time. The sun reflected off of the oily surface and threw up a scent that reminded the major of time spent in theme parks and on walking trails.

Twisted piles of former cars stretched for half a mile down both shoulders of the road to create an iron canyon. The next traveler to find the site might see it as a sign of hope. Perhaps thinking that a reconstituted government had reorganized to the point of assigning road crews.

The major knew better. There was no hope. Whatever optimism he had once had for a new world had faded with the passing of his wife and grandson. Since then, life had been only a brutal struggle to survive. Often, he questioned his own persistence. He had lost two sons and a daughter-in-law during the apocalypse. The passing of his wife and grandson a year later removed from him all personal interest in living.

He supposed he had a new family to protect, but they were no substitute. In the end, he always attributed his pursuit of survival to his stubborn nature. His wife used to tease him about it. It looked like she was right.

"We found a rig a few miles down the road, sir. The tires should be here soon." The runner's voice pulled him from his musings and back to the road before him.

"The path is clear?"

The runner nodded. "We've scouted to within sight of the town. The road is clear all the way to the gates."

"What's the status of the town?"

"It looks like they're ready for us, sir."

The major smiled. "Wake them up."

The runner saluted and dashed ahead of the major to the prison car. Striking a crowbar against the slats of the livestock trailer sent a clatter through the cage that the prisoners could not ignore. The captives awoke in a panic. Those near the slats sprang back, trying to save or comfort bashed fingers and ringing ears.

The runner slid the crowbar back into his belt. "The major will now speak!"

The major strode to the midpoint of the trailer and surveyed his audience. In some eyes he still saw rage, but generally it was fear. Fear was necessary, but he had hoped to alleviate some of it. He had replaced the shredded eye patch to hide his disfigurement, but there was little he could do to hide the healing wound on his face. They stared in disgust and terror.

The raspy voice did less to soothe them. Wheezes and squeaks like the final gasp of the dying brought his message to the prisoners.

"Ladies, gentlemen, and children, welcome. You are guests of the mighty nation of Alasis, the most powerful nation in the former United States. The power you see before you is a fraction of our empire. It is a vast nation, and you have been selected to become citizens.

"Each of you will enjoy a security that your former home could not provide you. Our nation will provide you with comfort, food, and a steady economy. You, in turn, will pledge your loyalty, your labor, and your love to Alasis.

"We don't wish to harm you. We wish to welcome you, with open arms, into our family. We have one more community to liberate from the brutalities of the wasteland; then we will return to your home.

"I hope that in the time we have left on the road you will reflect on your good fortune. You've been accepted into a wondrous new beginning, a chance to rebuild the world that man's gluttony and greed destroyed.

"Alasis is mankind's best chance at building a world that can survive.

"Thank you for your time."

With this, the major stepped away from the trailer full of prisoners, wondering if even he believed a word he had said. Alasis was the most powerful and organized city-state on the continent. Whether acceptance into its walls was a blessing or a curse, however, even he couldn't be certain.

# 27

A belief in the power of concrete and modernization had caused the Downtown district of Dallas to pave over most things green or old. It wasn't until the renaissance trends of the late 2000s that the planners decided to develop green spaces within the city. This exceptional lack of plant life worked in the post-apocalyptic travelers' favor.

The growth accelerant had few large trees or park spaces to affect. This left only office plants and landscape shrubbery to absorb the agent. Had more green space been available, the growth would have made the Dallas streets impassable. Instead, lucky bamboo, bonsai trees, and ivy vines that had been abandoned on desktops and windowsills absorbed the chemical. These office plants erupted from their planters and burst through skyscraper windows to drape a canopy of green over the former business district.

It was also unfortunate that the apocalypse occurred on Valentine's Day. Massive rose bushes had shattered ornate vases, plummeted from office buildings, and taken root in the city's storm drains. Stems as thick as trees rose from crumbled sidewalks and bloomed with massive roses tinted the sunlight hues of red and yellow.

The Silver Lining crashed through the creeping vines. Snapping like gunfire, the vines left sap and pulp across the body of the motor coach. Leaves and spores poured through the open windshield, covering the dash.

Alex flinched as branches and vines jutted in and out of the shattered windshield. He brushed the seedlings from his eyes quickly, struggling to keep both hands on the shotgun.

Small vines snapped away at the mass of the coach, while the thicker ones caused the vehicle to lurch and bounce as it made its way down the street.

Jerry fought the wheel, wrestling the coach from their grasp. He marveled at the growth. It was much thicker than he had last seen it. The canopy had lowered and threatened to touch the ground in several places.

Inside the coach, the passengers were thrown from their seats during a hard left. Jerry demanded everything from the engine as he maneuvered deftly through the streets. Though it seemed random to his passengers, the route he took through the city kept the vehicle clear of the few parks and patches of grass in the area.

He hadn't forgotten the streets. Despite the frantic steering, he kept his bearings, always moving south and east to reach a ramp up on the elevated safety of Highway 45.

"What was that?" Alex sat up, his grip on the shotgun tightened.

Jerry followed the barrel and looked into the street.

"What?"

Alex peered into the dense growth coming from the lobby of one of Dallas's many nondescript office buildings. "I guess it was nothing."

"Keep watching." Jerry sped up.

A chorus of faint, high-pitched whines penetrated the truck as countless vines scratched against its skin. Those heavier with water slapped against the truck, splattering the moisture across the body and in through the bullet holes.

"There!" Alex pointed with the shotgun.

Jerry saw the movement. It moved quickly, blending into the shadows of the jungle. He didn't see it clearly, but its shape was human.

"Shit."

The figure had disappeared to the left. He turned right on Harwood Street and out from under the skyscrapers. The properties along this road had been concrete lots and low-rise buildings. Few plants took root in the deserted parking lots. Soon, the only vegetation in sight was the grass growing between the seams of the pavement.

The rush of the tires on the road hushed as he sped down the grass-covered street. The steering wheel felt loose and the tires plowed down the long blades, but the ride inside the coach had improved. The highway was just ahead and he allowed himself a thought of relief.

The shadowy figure had not been alone. There was a flurry of motion on the street. Vague forms dashed about the field beside the coach. Soon, the dashing stopped and the creatures began to stand up.

They were everywhere.

As tall as a man, hundreds of them began to appear. They looked identical; each had a sickly green complexion and a haunted look in its eyes. Their dead gaze did not follow the coach.

"What are they?" Alex began to panic. "They aren't human."

"Not anymore." Jerry pressed the pedal harder and wished that he had spent more time souping up the Silver Lining's engine.

The creatures stood their ground; their only movement was a gentle sway as if blown by a breeze. More creatures appeared as the coach sped south down Harwood.

"What are they doing?" Erica screamed from the back.

"Scaring us."

"It's working." She had her arm around Austin. Pulling the costume's head down tight with both hands, the young boy shook in his bear suit.

"Oh my God!" Alex pointed to the right.

The old mason hall had stood empty for years, even before the evacuation of the Metroplex. The art deco building was massive. Twin steel doors, two stories tall, had burst open. More of the creatures rushed down the stairs into the sunlight.

Buds protruded from their skin. Vines drooped from the backs and arms of some.

They rushed into the street as the coach flew by the ornate steps of the Shriner hall. They gave chase.

"What are they?"

"They're plants. Mean ones. Keep that gun in the window!"

The mob of altered plant life didn't chatter or roar. It screeched. Each creature emitted a sound that caused the passengers to cover their ears. Jerry had always associated the sound with spring. As they shrieked, he envisioned himself with a blade of grass to his lips —gently blowing to make it whistle.

But the creatures' sound was louder and more intense than any blade of grass.

The off ramp he planned to use to get on the highway wasn't far now. He blew through dormant intersections and kept his eye on the service road ahead.

A green wall descended in the coach's path. Hundreds of the creatures fell into place behind one another to form a field of green.

"Hold on!" He didn't slow; his foot never left the pedal.

The shrieks became unbearable as the coach plowed into the creatures. They splattered and smeared on the motor coach. They flew in all directions from the impact. Green ooze splattered through the broken windshield.

Alex recoiled into his seat.

"Alex! Shoot!"

The boy opened his eyes to see living vines reaching for him. He screamed and began to fire. Each shot spread more green pulp into the cab.

He fired until the gun was empty. A hand reached forward and pulled the shotgun from his grip and set another in its place. Erica and Trent reloaded the empty shotgun as Alex emptied the replacement.

The truck slowed from the resistance of the crowd. The tires lost traction as they slipped on the pulp of the crushed monsters.

All forward motion stopped.

Alex continued to blast any creatures that tried to climb the hood.

Jerry cranked the wheel left and spun the tires until they burned through the shrieking mass and touched the road again. The vehicle lurched under the canopy of the old Farmer's Market.

Here the surface of the road was exposed; he could get solid traction and build some momentum.

But there was no time. The mob of living plants surrounded them. The creatures amassed on all sides of the home and began to rock the coach.

Alex fired another shotgun dry. Erica handed him a fresh one.

Jerry drew the .45s and emptied a magazine from each, picking off a creature with each shot.

"Do something!" Erica screamed.

He risked a glance to the back of the cab. Erica's fingers bled. He couldn't tell if she had been hit or worn the flesh from her hands feeding shells into shotguns.

Trent had grabbed a weapon of his own and was firing at the creatures as they began to shatter the windows. Chewy barked ferociously and snapped at any vines that made their way into the interior. She snatched one in her teeth and thrashed her head until the vine detached from its host.

Jerry emptied another mag and grabbed for the iPod. He held the button until it chimed ready for a voice command. He yelled into the device, but it didn't register over the growing peel of shrieks.

He tried again, this time cupping his hand to block out everything but his voice.

"Play sequence, Ring of Fire!"

A chime rang through the coach's surround system and the device's voice replayed the command.

"Playing songs by The Muppets."

"What? No! No!" He mashed the button harder to reset the voice prompt as *Mahna, Mahna* began to play.

The song filled the cabin as the Silver Lining shook violently. Cracks began to appear in the shell. Curtain rods crashed down. Kitchen drawers rattled open and spilled their contents onto the floor.

The iPod chimed again and Jerry spoke the command once more, "Play sequence, Ring of Fire."

Responding with a positive beep, the iPod displayed a picture of the legendary singer and Johnny Cash came over the stereo speakers. External speakers popped to life and the trumpets began to play. Soon, the Man-in-Black's voice boomed under the metal roof of the Farmer's Market.

"This isn't helping!" Erica began to cry. Her reloads were slowing.

"Wait for it." Jerry fired several more rounds through the windshield.

The chorus quickly approached.

"Everyone get away from the windows. Don't touch the walls." He dove to the back, dragging Alex with him.

The chorus erupted over the speakers.

On the exterior of the coach, spring loaded nozzles revealed themselves, each extending exactly twenty-eight degrees. Propane shot through pipes from the rear mounted tanks and hissed as it primed the system.

With a tremendous whoosh, the gas ignited. The nozzles spewed flames in a cyclone of fire around the Silver Lining as Johnny Cash went down, down, down.

The shrieks changed from bloodlust to pain as the creatures ignited and burned. The odor of charred flesh and burning cedar filled the air as the fire spread throughout the mob of creatures.

The flamethrower went cold, but the Man-in-Black kept singing.

Jerry slapped Alex on the back. "Get back on the window."

Alex leapt back in the passenger seat and shoved away two burning creatures that had chosen the hood of the coach to perform their death throes.

Jerry jumped back behind the wheel.

The majority of the burning creatures fled in no particular direction. Any that had escaped the burn-off watched the coach cautiously. Their shrieking stopped and the streets of Dallas were quiet.

The song reached its second chorus.

The remaining creatures scattered.

Johnny Cash continued to fill the former Farmer's Market. With the mob having dissipated, the overwhelming volume of the song became apparent.

Erica smiled. The boys darted about the cabin, peering out each window.

"They're all gone." Trent moved from window to window, not quite understanding what had happened.

"What's with the music?" Erica screamed to be heard. "What did you do?"

Jerry smiled. "Learned behavior. They won't come near us again during the chorus." Jerry fumbled for the iPod and stopped the music.

That's when they heard it.

"Librarian." The voice was low, raspy. "Librarian." It was weak. "Is that you, Librarian?" It sounded like a helpless old man calling for help, and it terrified him more than anything else on the planet.

---

## 28

A dull thud answered back as he kicked each of the new tires. Two were almost bald and one had been patched, but each now held air and supported the rig and its many trailers.

Satisfied with the "they'll do for now" explanation he had received from the engineer, the major ordered to have it noted that armored tires should be a priority project once the men returned to Alasis. The man who had fired on them had been a remarkable marksman, but others in the waste could get lucky. The search for spares had cost them a day. And each day meant that rations and supplies dwindled.

It was noted and the engineer stepped back to his post in the command center.

The major gave the tire one more swift kick and looked up at the wall of the trailer. The eyes of a child caught his. The girl was young —young enough to outgrow the memory of the horrors of what he and his men had done to the town of Vita Nova.

Years ago, the look on her face, like someone had pissed on her pony, would have stirred pangs of guilt. Years ago, there was no way he would have been able to raze a town or incarcerate innocent women and children. But times had changed. He was not the man he was years ago.

He smiled at the little girl who only stared back at him. "What's your name, little girl?"

The girl didn't make a sound. She just stared at him with big eyes of innocence. He could feel the gaze pass his eye and peer deep inside him. There was a discomfort that he welcomed. Guilt had resurfaced. It was a terrifying and invigorating feeling. It quickly overcame him and he began to plead with the girl.

"I'm doing this for your own good, sweetheart. The world is too dangerous. I'm taking you to a safer place."

Brown eyes stared back.

The major grabbed the slat and pulled himself to the little girl's level. "Can't you see that?"

The little girl, as cute as she was obnoxious, sighed and said, "I can see fine. You're the one with only one eye."

The guilt ebbed and disappeared. He reached through the slats and tried to grab the little girl. She easily ducked the awkward grasp and backed away from his reach.

"Get back here, you little brat. I'll slap some respect into you."

A woman's face appeared before him. Throwing herself between the major and the little girl, she fumed at the one-eyed monster. "Don't you talk to her like that, you bastard."

The major grabbed the woman by her hair and pulled her face into the grated wall so it was close to his.

"Don't you talk like that. This will be the last time I show compassion." He pushed her back from the wall just far enough to slap her across the face. The woman shrieked and fell back. The brown-eyed little girl rushed to her and put her arms around her.

He smiled at her again, but bared his teeth this time.

"I hope someone kills you good," said the little girl.

The major laughed and walked back to the cab. He climbed inside and moments later the rig belched a fury of black exhaust. The chassis rumbled on the frame as the monstrous truck was forced into gear. Chains rattled as the four trailers joined the forward surge down the road to New Hope.

# 29

There was a rustling about the motor coach. It was still outside. The creatures that weren't burning had fled. The raspy voiced continued.

"You always did like that song, Librarian. You played it constantly, safe inside your little hole."

The voice seemed to come from all around them. Erica and the boys looked to Jerry. He wasn't moving.

"Jerry? Jerry?" Erica shook his shoulder. He remained still.

The older boys saw this and clutched their weapons tight. Peering out the windows, they tried to spot the unseen enemy. They saw nothing.

"And the louder I pounded on the door, the louder you would play your tunes, Librarian."

Austin crouched on the floor and felt secure in his bear suit.

There was a violent rustling. The coach shook as vines quickly entangled the vehicle like tentacles, rushing across the windows as the structure of the vehicle creaked. Light faded in the cabin as the vines fully encompassed the coach.

"Jerry?"

There was no reaction.

The movement of the vines continued. They were quick. Each

moved so fast that detail was indistinguishable. Erica spun, looking from window to window for any indication of what was attacking them. She saw it.

Its face dragged across a window of the Silver Lining. The skin was thick and brown as if grown of bark. The eyes were not lifeless like the other creatures; these eyes were sharp and darted back and forth, scanning the interior looking for their prey.

The voice spoke again, "Ah, it is you, Librarian. I never thought I'd see you again. We have so much catching up to do. Why don't you come out?"

Chewy bristled and began to bark.

"And your little dog too. I've really missed him since that day."

This jarred Jerry from his frozen state.

"We have nothing to talk about. We're just passing through."

"Oh, I don't think so, Librarian. This is my city. You saw to that. Didn't you?"

"You know that wasn't my choice. The door was time locked."

The volume of the voice rose, but it still sounded faint, like a fierce burst of wind through a tree with only so many leaves to rustle. "Liar!"

The motor coach rocked up on two wheels. It slammed back to the ground. The occupants were thrown off balance and each grasped for support.

"You locked me out. You made me this. You took my humanity!"

"There was nothing I could do," Jerry pleaded. "I would have saved you if I could."

"You can't save anybody, Librarian."

The window above the sofa shattered. Vines poured into the cabin. The thick roots moved like snakes and encircled Erica around the waist. She screamed as the vines ripped her from the vehicle.

Jerry roared; rage filled his scream. He sprung from his seat and rushed to the rear door. It wouldn't open. He threw his weight against it. It didn't give. Vines held it shut.

Frantic, he tore open a closet door. He grabbed a machete that lay on the floor and rushed back to the front of the motor home. He snatched the shotgun from Alex's hand, crashed shoulder first through the windshield, and rolled into the street.

Chewy scurried over the seats and through the broken glass after her friend and master.

The creature had gotten bigger.

When Jerry had first emerged from the shelter, the creature was little bigger than the man it had been. The transformation from man to plant had increased his bulk. Vines had only begun to sprout from his arms back then. Now they sprouted from his entire body and writhed like sentient creatures.

The beast's skin had been dry and scaly seven years ago. It had cracked and hardened a thousand times since that day to form a dense bark that appeared completely bulletproof. For every crack, the creature's height and mass had increased.

It stood twelve feet tall at what Jerry assumed was the shoulder; countless vines reached three times that into the air. The shape of the human that it had once been could barely be distinguished from the myriad vines.

"There you are," the beast rasped.

Erica continued to scream. She tried to grab at the vines about her waist, but the violent thrashing forced her limbs to flail helplessly.

"Put her down!"

"Or what? You'll read me a fairy tale?"

Before he had tried to drown out the man's constant pounding with music, and after he had pleaded with the man to find help elsewhere, Jerry had read to him from inside the shelter. He did this to calm a man he thought was dying, but the stories only caused the man to beat harder against the reinforced steel door.

A vine wrapped around Jerry's ankle. Jerry swung the machete and severed the vine.

Chewy held several more vines at bay, catching the occasional growth in her jaws and tearing it to pieces.

"I've got more vines than you have swings in your puny arms, Librarian."

Jerry slid the machete into his belt and held up the shotgun. He charged toward the body of the creature, firing into the mass of vines that tried to grab him. A substantial enough hit caused each vine to go limp. But there was always another to replace it.

Jerry ran out of shells fast. He dropped the gun and drew the machete. Hacking his way closer to the body of the beast, he screamed as he sliced his way closer.

One of the thicker vines struck him across the chest and drove him against the coach. He landed hard on his tailbone.

"For six months I beat on that door and begged for you to let me in."

A second vine launched at him like a spear. Jerry fell out of the way. The vine grazed his cheek and embedded itself into the quarter panel.

"But you were too scared to help a fellow human."

Jerry regained his feet and charged again.

Leaves and vines fell to the ground as he struck them. Hacking and chopping, he managed to kill several, but there were too many. He had not even come within striking distance of the creature's body when several vines ensnared his feet and pulled him to the ground. He was overcome as countless more vines entwined his arms.

"And when you finally came out, what did you do? You tried to kill me. You caged me and left me to die."

Jerry struggled, "You tried to kill us first."

"You deserved it! Me? Not as much. Hadn't I suffered enough?"

Chewy rushed to aid the fallen nomad. The mighty dog tore at the vines that held her friend fast. Vines launched toward her and she was soon caught within the living jungle of the creature's mutation.

Jerry was lifted from the ground. He gripped the machete tight, but he could not move his arms. He had no leverage. Whenever he managed to wrestle his grip free, other vines intercepted the blade and prevented the warrior from taking a full swing.

The creature drew him closer until the two were face to face.

"Finally," it rasped. "With every pound I cursed you. With every bud I pictured your death at my hands."

From inside the flurry of vines, a hand, a human hand, emerged and wrapped around Jerry's throat.

"The fairy tale is over, Librarian."

"Grrrrr!"

The creature turned his gaze to the motor coach. Three bears, small, medium, and large sizes, had emerged from the vehicle.

The creature looked back at Jerry and laughed. "Oh, my. Grizzlies. I'm going to kill you and finish off the three bears. But her?" He moved Erica close so Jerry could see her. "I think I'll keep her alive for, oh, six months."

Jerry spit on the creature's barely human face.

"Keep it up, Librarian. I love the rain now." The creature turned suddenly. He dropped his hand from Jerry's throat and began to thrash and stumble.

Jerry looked back to the coach.

The three boys, dressed as bears, assaulted the creature on three fronts. The blades affixed to their paws tore through the vines.

The creature grabbed them, but struggled to hold them. The suits were loose enough that any grip on the costume left the boys room to wriggle their wrists free.

They worked together slashing at the creature's many serpentine limbs. Vines fell dormant all around them. If one of the bears fell, a brother was there to pick him up while the third held the vines at bay.

Jerry felt the grip on his wrists loosen. The boys divided the creature's focus. If they kept it up, he might have a chance.

Austin roared as he attacked the plant. A vine engulfed his head and began to squeeze. He dropped to the ground, leaving the mask behind. Just as quick, he stood up and struck down the vines that held his bear head.

"You little shits." There was rage in the rasp now. The collected cadence was gone. The creature stumbled backward and began to use its vines for defense instead of attack. It threw up walls of brown roots and leafy screens to protect itself.

The boys' bear claws cut easily through the vegetation. The blades were sharp and they were small enough that the surrounding vines could not interfere with their work.

The vine holding Jerry's left hand was needed for defense. Jerry gripped the machete tighter in his right hand and drew a knife from his pocket with his left. With one flick, the blade exposed itself.

Jerry spoke. "Phillip."

Hearing his human name spoken for the first time in years, the creature turned back to face him.

The former librarian drove the knife in the creature's eye.

It screamed in its demon-toned rasp and reeled back. The vines released their grasp.

Jerry fell to the ground in a crouch and rushed in, brandishing the machete.

The boys continued their assault; claws flashed, pulp dripped, and vines fell.

Jerry fought his way to the man inside the creature, taking huge slashes at his chest. It threw up its arm to defend itself. Jerry hacked through bark-thick skin into flesh, blood, and bone.

Chewy was now at his side, her massive jowls locked around the creature's leg, pushing it further off balance.

It dropped Erica and brought its last few remaining vines into the fight.

The boys made quick work of them.

Roars of rage grew from inside the plant creature and turned to shrieks of pain as the vines fell and the man in the bushes emerged.

Chewy twisted her head and pulled its leg out from beneath it to bring Jerry and the creature face to face.

It began to laugh. "You can't kill me, Librarian. My roots—"

The machete slashed through the creature's head, exposing, to everyone's surprise, brain, not pulp.

The creature's eyes went blank. Its vines collapsed. It fell over dead.

Austin continued to growl at the fallen limbs.

Jerry rushed to Erica. She was hurt, but she was alive. He helped her to her feet. She stood, clasping her side. Her waist was bruised and scratched from where the vines had assaulted her.

She threw her arms around Jerry. He hurt as well. His limbs felt as if they had been stretched beyond their limit and were just now settling back into place.

"I'm sorry," she said as she held him tight. "I'm sorry."

"It's okay." Jerry held her close.

"I've been horrible to you."

"It's okay."

"How can you say that? After the way I treated you?"

"You didn't know."

"But—"

"Erica, the first time we met I dove headfirst into a wall. I'm not sure that I would have trusted me either. And I know me fairly well."

She started to cry and buried her face in his shoulder.

He pulled her closer and stroked her hair.

When he finally looked up, he had an audience. Alex was grinning, Trent made lewd gestures, and Austin hid in his bear suit.

"Good work, bear brigade. You boys just saved our lives."

Alex blushed. The smallest just stayed in his bear suit and saluted.

"Let's go guys. We've got to keep moving."

Chewy sat at his feet and panted. Jerry petted her head and looked at Erica. "You too, girls. We've got to get to that town before that truck does."

"Hey," Trent said, "before we go, could you never call us the bear brigade ever again?"

"Get on the truck, Trent."

# 30

---

The people of New Hope gathered before him. Strain from days of defense preparations had left them worn and tired. Several dozed while others batted their eyes in veiled attempts to stay awake. Logan paced the front of the room as everyone found their seats. All but the sentries had been called to the town hall barn.

Behind Logan was a map of the town, an aerial view that showed the walls of the city and where defensive positions would be taken. Archers were denoted by arrows, which seemed obvious to Logan, but the symbol took three votes and a compromise with the flamethrower committee to be accepted as the "little symbol thingy" that would tell the archers where to stand. The compromise was that the flamethrower teams would be referred to as fire people instead of firemen and would be indicated on the map as a dove, because a flame seemed too violent. Medics chose ambulances instead of crosses in case some of the attackers were of a different belief system than the people of New Hope.

A gnarled pool cue served as his pointer. As the last person sat, he banged it against the wall to get the room's attention. It could never be used to shoot a game of pool again, but it was perfect for planning the defense of a walled town against the onslaught of merciless villains in a giant armored truck.

"Now, when the lookout spots the truck—"

The door to the town hall barn burst open.

"The truck is coming!" the young lookout panted.

The citizens of New Hope began to panic.

Logan bashed the cue against the steel wall. Thunder roared inside the town hall barn. "Calm down, everyone. You all know what to do."

Various voices in the crowd responded:

"No, we don't."

"You hadn't started."

"Am I an arrow or a fireman?"

"Fire-person!"

"Whatever."

Logan snapped the pool cue over his knee. The crack bounced off the walls and silenced the crowd. "Just get to your positions."

The town hall barn emptied. Logan took the lead and scaled a fabricated ladder to the outer wall of the town with ease. The people followed. Some hesitated. Others stayed close to Logan.

The citizen soldiers grabbed tie-rod crossbows, shouldered rifles, or manned flamethrower turrets. Medics took position in doorways, ready to run to the aid of the fallen. Logan jumped from his perch to the roof of the cement truck as it rolled into place.

Carl stepped from the cab.

"Gadgeteer!" Logan yelled down to the small round man.

The town's gadget man looked up and smiled at hearing this. He gave Logan an enthusiastic thumbs up and an air fist bump. Logan held out his hand.

Carl threw an air high five. Logan stomped his foot on the hood, "It means throw me the keys, you idiot."

Carl was surprised at the outburst, but obediently dug into his pocket and tossed the keys to Logan.

The warrior grabbed them out of the air and stepped back onto the ledge that surrounded the wall. Pacing, his pistol in hand, he spoke to the people below him.

He turned his back to the wasteland and did his best to prepare the people for the coming horror.

"Remember," he shouted to the town. "The truck is most likely armored. Do not fire at the truck. Its walls are impenetrable. You must wait for the men to disembark."

"It doesn't look that armored," a woman holding a crossbow argued.

"Looks can be deceiving."

"It looks like it's about to fall apart," an older man said.

"He said it was huge. It's not that big." This began a chorus of doubt that moved up and down the walls.

"There can't be more than a few men in there."

"Is that a Winnebago?"

"I don't see the W."

"I don't think they all have Ws."

Logan turned to see a cloud of dust approaching.

"Bookworm?" he said under his breath. He yelled to the crowd, "Hold your fire. It's not them."

"How is that thing holding together?" The crowd continued to chatter as the motor coach pulled up to the gates of the town.

"Bookworm?" Logan shouted to the coach. With the windshield shattered, he could see the mastiff in the passenger seat. Chewy growled.

Jerry stepped from the coach and stood before the town. "Good people of the town of New Hope, you are in danger."

"Really, asshole? What do you think we're all doing up on the wall? Dumb ass."

The young man was grabbed by an ear and dragged off of the wall. "Jefferson Davis Allen, you watch your mouth!"

"Logan is a fraud." Jerry pointed to the warrior on the wall.

"You're the fraud, Bookworm," Roy Tinner shouted back. "Logan told us all about you, library boy."

"Jerry." Logan stepped in front of the agitated crowd. "You should go. It's not safe here."

"I never would have guessed it, Logan. It was you all along."

"Jerry, take your girlfriend. And your … bears? And go."

Jerry turned to see his companions behind him. The boys still wore their bear costumes. Each was covered in grass stains.

"How many towns, Logan? How many since Colorado?"

"Jerry, it's for your own good. Leave while you still can." Logan's mutt was at his heel, growling at the group. Chewy burst through the front of the Silver Lining, put herself between the dog and her master, and growled back.

"How many lives have you destroyed? How many people have trusted you, only to be betrayed?"

"I can't be responsible for your safety, Bookworm."

"I'm not leaving, Logan." Jerry stepped closer to the wall and addressed the crowd. "Good people, this man has sold you a lie. You are not safe behind your walls."

"He's protecting us," Roy pushed Logan out of the way and held up the crossbow as proof of his statement.

"Roy, don't." Logan tried to calm the councilman.

"They're fake," Jerry fired back.

"I'll show you fake, you ..." Roy Tinner lowered the crossbow and aimed it Jerry.

"Roy, stop!" Logan screamed.

Jerry stood his ground. "Shoot me, Roy!"

"Jerry, no!" Erica rushed to his side.

He pushed her back and turned back to Roy.

"C'mon, Roy. Pull the trigger, you spineless paper pusher."

Logan put his hand on the crossbow, but he was too late. Roy pulled the release and fired the bolt straight at Jerry's chest.

Erica screamed. Chewy barked. Jerry didn't move.

The bolt whistled through the air, struck against the grain of Jerry's leather jacket and shattered.

Roy stared in disbelief.

Jerry held up his hands. "Still don't believe me, Roy?"

Roy grabbed the crossbow from a man standing next to him and fired again with the same result. Splintered wood bounced at Jerry's feet.

"You see, it's ..."

Roy grabbed another bow and fired.

The bolt shattered.

"Okay, Roy. I think I've made my point."

Roy, the city councilman, asked for another crossbow.

"They're all the same. Don't you see?"

Another bolt shattered against his jacket.

"Would you stop it, Roy?" Jerry stepped forward. The pile of brittle wood cracked beneath his feet.

"It's going to be the same with flamethrowers. Maybe one good burst and they'll suddenly lose pressure. You've dug pitfalls around the walls, correct?"

One of the defenders nodded.

"They won't go for the walls. They'll go straight for the gate. And Logan will let them in."

Carl stepped forward. "Not this baby. She's a beast with a hardened load in the back." Carl giggled and looked to Logan for approval.

"Who has the keys?"

Without hesitation, Carl pointed at Logan.

There was a sudden burst of flame from one of the cannons. A roar of approval went up from the fire-person team. The jet of flame sputtered and fizzled; so did the roar of approval.

Roy had watched the pyrotechnic display and was finally convinced. He turned to accuse Logan, but the man had disappeared.

"Find him!" The mayor gripped his daughter close.

The town walls emptied as the people searched for the man they had trusted.

Jerry heard shouts and gunfire. Then, all was quiet. The town was still. The cement truck fired up and began to move.

Roy, the city councilman, stepped from the gates and waved Jerry and his friends into New Hope.

# 31

---

The air brakes fired in quick succession and the massive rig began to squeal as the calipers struggled to halt the forward momentum of the four trailers.

A lone rider sat astride his motorcycle. A second bike was propped up next to him. The rider waited for the rig to come to a stop before he yelled over the thrumming of the engine, "Apple Pie Sucks!"

The pass phrase was accepted. Doors flew open as the guard detail disembarked and secured a perimeter around the truck. Once it was established, two of the guards rushed to the bikes.

The rider dismounted and jogged to the rig as the guards fired up the motorcycles and pulled them into the rear trailer.

The rider pulled himself into the command center and saluted the major.

"Report, Sergeant." The raspy voice seemed tired. He didn't look up from the map table.

"Sir. Logan brought a woman to the rendezvous. Williams and I fired on the car with live rounds as ordered. As planned, Logan pursued us and discharged several blanks. I fell. Logan and the woman then pursued Williams over a mile up the road."

The rider stopped.

The major looked up. "And?"

"When I was able to check, I found Williams dead. Shot, sir."

"Logan?"

"I can't be certain, sir. Perhaps the girl. I found a bloody knife near the body. I'm quite certain the staged knife fight occurred."

The major considered this information; his eye drifted up and to the right. "It's hard to trust a con man, Sergeant. He could be working an angle."

"What's the angle, sir?"

"I can't be certain. But that man is always working an angle. Maybe he finally found a place he wanted to settle down."

The sergeant couldn't see it. Logan wasn't one to settle down. He had shown up half dead at the gates of Alasis and conned his way in. Even the most developed city in the Midwest hadn't swayed the vagabond's wanderlust.

"Either way," the major continued, "the cells are full. It may be best to approach this town with a no-prisoner approach."

"Sir?"

"No prisoners, Sergeant. Spread the order."

"But, sir, what about Logan?"

"That slippery bastard will be smart enough to keep his head down. If not, I'm fairly certain we can find some other scumbag drifter that will fit the part."

The sergeant hesitated.

"That's an order about the orders, Sergeant."

The pondering ceased and the soldier snapped to attention. He stepped from the cab and spread the word that no prisoners were to be taken from the town of New Hope.

The major pulled a microphone from a control panel and flipped a switch that enabled the loudspeaker. He cleared his throat and spoke into the microphone.

"It's been a good season, boys. And, from what Logan tells us, this place is packed with food and medical supplies. More than enough to bring home to our growing family.

"After this final raid, we'll head home and celebrate. Do me proud, boys."

Through the hull of the truck he could hear the cheers of his men. Wars may change, worlds may change, but soldiers are always happy to go home.

He turned the amplifier off and turned to the driver. "Let's roll out. And if you see that bastard in the Winnebago, you run his ass off the road."

"Yes, sir."

# 32

There was no fanfare. No crowds, no throngs of grateful citizens rushed the Silver Lining. Roy walked slowly ahead of the coach and guided it to the middle of the town. The Silver Lining jiggled; riddled with bullet holes, cracked from constricting vines, its structure had been weakened. A quick drive from Dallas that had disregarded potholes and all but the largest pieces of debris had accelerated the decay of the coach.

Jerry pulled close to the town hall barn in the center of town and shifted into park. Before he could stand, Erica was out the door and charging toward where the town had bound Logan against an old lamppost. Jerry stepped from the cabin in time to see her strike him across the face. She drew her arm back for another blow when two of the townspeople rushed in and held her back.

"Let go of me!" She kicked as they dragged her back and ground her heels into the brown dirt of Town Square.

Jerry ran up to the struggle.

"This man murdered my family!" She spit at Logan.

Logan shrugged. Blotches of purple welts blended into the scars on his face. His mouth bled from a missing tooth and he panted deeply. Still, he grinned.

Jerry ripped the hands of the townspeople from her arms and waist. Trying to calm her, he took her hands in his and tried to see past the rage in her eyes.

"Erica, Erica, Erica," he pleaded to get her attention away from anger; she was hysterical and would not look at him. He shook her gently by the shoulders. Finally she looked into his eyes. There was calm there. He stared into her gaze for a moment, released her hands and said, "Knock that grin off of his face, please."

She smiled and returned to kicking and slapping the bound man. Logan moaned as she drove her feet into his ribs. He shrieked as she punched him in the face.

The citizens rushed in again, but Jerry stood between them and the beating. "Guys, why not?"

The people of New Hope pondered the question for a moment, looked to one another, shrugged and walked away.

Jerry grabbed one by the arm. "Where's the mayor?"

"Here." The man strode over to Jerry and cast only a glance at the girl beating the man they once trusted. "Thank God you showed up when you did."

"Actually, I showed up earlier." Jerry looked to Roy, who was only steps behind the mayor.

"Roy!"

Roy began to stammer. Jerry cut him off.

"It doesn't matter, you don't have much time." He was interrupted by a loud groan from Logan.

"You son of a bitch!" Erica had Logan by the hair and was driving his head against the post repeatedly.

The two men stepped a few feet away. Erica's curses and Logan's grunts provided the ambient sounds for the conversation.

"The truck will be on its way by now." Jerry pointed in the truck's general direction.

The mayor had always done his best to appear a fearless leader, but now, his composure was lost. "Our defenses are useless."

"You're not going to need them ..."

"Little-prick bastard." Erica's insults began coming with heavier breaths.

Logan groaned and lost another tooth.

Jerry crossed the courtyard to get away from the noise.

The mayor followed close behind, pleading for an answer to the situation. "How will we protect the town?"

"You won't."

"I don't understand."

Jerry finally spotted what he needed across the courtyard. "Does that pickup run?"

"Yes."

"Good, I'll need three men. You should probably make it ones you don't like very much."

"Now, hold on ..."

"Your defenses are rigged. Your weapons are crap. You can't defend this town. The only chance is to stop the truck before it gets here."

A new style of swearing came from behind them. The two men turned to see that Sarah had joined Erica and was helping her beat Logan. The mayor made a move to stop her. Jerry waved it off. "Let her help. Erica's hand has got to be getting sore by now."

The mayor nodded.

"Now, have three men meet me by my coach and get that pickup running."

The mayor agreed and started barking names to the crowd that had gathered around them.

Jerry pulled Erica and Sarah off of Logan. He received a few kicks for the effort, but the girls relented. Logan had collapsed to the ground; only his shackled hands kept him from being a heap on the ground. Still, he laughed, while grinning through broken teeth and busted lips.

"You're dead, Bookworm. You can't stop us now."

Jerry took a knee in front of the con man.

"I don't know what these people are going to do to you. But I do know that I'm not going to stop them. How many people have died at your hands? How many towns razed?"

"We're all just trying to survive out here."

"Not all of us."

"You should have seen the look on your face when we marched into that town in Colorado. Everything started breaking. All of your plans collapsing." Logan laughed. "That look was better than the score we took that day."

"I'm going to stop them, Logan. No one else will die because of you."

Jerry turned away. Logan spit blood after him.

Erica was doubled over crying. Her knuckles matched her bloody fingers. He put an arm around her and whispered in her ear, "Erica, it's going to be okay."

"How can you say that? You haven't lost what I have."

Jerry lifted her chin. "You haven't lost your family."

She mocked him, "Oh, sure, they'll always be with me as long they're in my heart."

"Not in your heart. In the trailer behind the truck."

Her eyes grew wide. She said nothing.

"They weren't killed. They were taken prisoner."

She began to sob and smile.

"I'm going to save them."

She looked at him through puffy eyes and hugged him, "I know you will." She kissed him on the cheek. She didn't linger, but there was warmth in her lips that held.

The mayor approached with Roy Tinner and the three volunteers: Carl Parker, Timothy Simmons, and the sheriff.

Roy stuck out his hand. "I would like to take this opportunity to apologize for my behavior when you first arrived."

"Fuck you, Roy. This is Erica. She was at a town called Vita Nova when the truck rolled through. Please take care of her and my three young friends here." The boys had finally emerged from the Silver Lining. Austin still wore his mask. The other two peeked out from behind the collars of their bear suits.

"The bears?" Roy asked.

"Yes, Roy, the bears. Why don't you start filling out some forms?" Jerry moved to the door of the coach.

Alex tugged at his elbow. "But we want to come with you."

Jerry put his hand on the boy's shoulder. "You boys have done enough. Stay here. Watch Chewy for me."

Jerry stepped into the coach and emerged a moment later with an armload of weapons and a belt slung over his shoulder. He called the three volunteers and began handing out weapons.

"Who's driving?"

Carl stepped forward and raised his hand. "The name's Carl, but people around here call me the Gadgeteer."

"No, they don't."

"Shut up, Timmy." Carl was disappointed the name hadn't caught on in the few days Logan was around.

A bulletproof vest struck the Gadgeteer in the face and fell into his hands.

"What's this?"

"Body armor."

Timothy, the whiny councilman, complained, "Why does he get body armor?"

"He needs to live the longest." Jerry checked his own weapons. Across his chest, he strapped an MP5 he had taken from an abandoned police station. The Colt 1911s were holstered at his waist.

"All right; two in the front and one in the back with me. We're going stop that truck."

## 33

The noise created by the massive semi could be heard for miles. Stealth wasn't a part of its arsenal. The four trailers rattled incessantly as they each found bumps and debris in the road.

The survivors of Vita Nova and two other towns, Hope Pointe and Point Hope, huddled in the prison car. Starving and broken, they no longer looked through the grates of the former pig trailer or at the landscape passing by at forty-five miles an hour.

They also didn't see the blue and white 4x4 launch up the shoulder of the road until it was right beside them.

"Everyone get to the back of the trailer!" Jerry screamed through the grates. He stood in the back of the pickup with one hand on the light bar and the other holding a .45.

A soldier appeared on top of the trailer ahead of the prison car and opened fire on the truck.

Carl swerved as the bullets began to pour down.

Jerry and the sheriff fired back. The soldier took a bullet in the leg and collapsed from the roof of the trailer. He didn't fall far. A safety harness snapped taut, slammed the soldier against the side of the trailer, and turned him upside down. Fighting against momentum and the harness itself, he struggled to right himself. His weapon fell to the highway and bounced underneath the wheel of the truck.

"Get to the back!" Jerry shouted again as the other man in the truck bed began firing at more soldiers that had appeared at the roofline of the trailer.

The prisoners were snapped from their stupor and began to rush to the back of the trailer.

Jerry tapped on the back of Carl's head and the truck sped up. They pulled next to the coupling arm of the prison trailer. Gunshots rang out around him as he holstered the gun and steadied himself to jump.

A right curve in the road caused the rig to veer. The pickup was forced to follow. The sudden turn threw Jerry off balance. He was forced to grab the light bar just to stay in the bed of the truck.

As the rig veered to follow the curve, the gun turret behind the plow caught sight of the pickup. The gunner frantically tried to turn the turret and fire on the 4 x 4. The road straightened before he could fire.

The first guard dangled by his safety harness and was struggling to pull himself between the two trailers and out of harm's way.

Jerry leaned down and yelled to Timothy through the missing window. "Watch that gunner!" Carl hunkered down behind the wheel, trying to hide his round figure behind the bulletproof vest.

Jerry found a rhythm in the sway of the pickup and made his leap. He crashed chest first across the spar that joined the prison car to the trailer in front of it.

His feet dangled and bounced against the passing ground. He could feel the texture of the asphalt through the leather of his boots. He struggled to pull himself up, while his allies in the truck continued to fire at the soldiers on the roof.

He turned his body and lay down on the spar. Staring into the sky, he saw two more soldiers leap onto the prison car to assist in the defense of the rig.

Jerry pulled himself up and unbuckled the blue belt he had grabbed from his armory. He slapped it around the spar and cinched it tight.

He signaled Carl, and the nose of the pickup dove as the driver slammed on the brakes. The plan was to draw the guard's attention by taking up position on the far side of the rig. A moment later, Jerry spied the blue and white paint through the gap in the trailers. The diversion would work as long as the guards were forced to keep their heads down.

Jerry yelled back to the prisoners, "Hold on to something!"

The prisoners responded by grabbing the sties and rails of the former livestock hauler. Jerry lit the fuse of the explosive belt and turned to climb the ladder of the command trailer.

There was no ladder. Why wasn't there a ladder? There was no way up. This was a major flaw in the plan.

He had to try to signal Carl. He shouted at the blue and white pickup; his cries were drowned out by the cacophony of gunfire and trailers.

The rig veered left and the nomad was thrown off balance again. A roar of gunfire erupted from the turret before the road straightened. The pickup became visible again; the hood was on fire. The sheriff continued to fire from the truck bed while Carl struggled to maintain control of the burning vehicle.

The fuse hissed at his feet.

He reached down and tried to unlatch the trailer door. He would face the odds of attacking the crew directly.

The latch had been removed.

Jerry banged on the door. He could feel his fists bruise as they struck the heavy gauge steel of the trailer. Panic manifested itself as coldness in his chest. The hissing got faster as the spark approached the point of detonation.

He continued to pound, hoping that some foolish soldier inside would think a comrade needed help. He heard nothing inside the door. He crouched, like a child hiding from a scolding, as the fuse approached the explosive belt.

From the corner of his eye he saw movement. The harnessed guard had finally gotten his hand on the edge of the trailer and was pulling himself around the corner.

Jerry jumped a second ahead of the fuse.

From the side of the trailer, the guard stuck his other hand around the corner. This was the arm that Jerry grabbed.

The trailer door flew open; armed soldiers inside the command trailer prepared to open fire.

The bomb exploded and Jerry swung away from the blast on the arm of the other man. Jerry's weight separated the guard's arm from his shoulder, but the appendage held.

The guard screamed and let go of the trailer. The pair swung clear of the blast.

The force of the explosion knocked the soldiers in the back of the command center off their feet. Several were killed instantly as the spar connecting the two trailers turned to shrapnel.

Both trailers were thrown into the air.

Jerry watched as the prison car successfully detached from the rig. Its severed coupling dug a trench into the black asphalt of the former state highway, throwing sparks and chunks of black tar everywhere.

Three guards who had been on the prison trailer were thrown more than fifty feet before they struck the black top and slid to a stop on their faces.

Two soldiers on the command trailer were tossed to the road below as the axle crashed back to the ground.

Jerry pulled himself, hand-over-hand, up the guard's dislocated arm and grabbed the harness. From here he was able to gain the top of the trailer after stepping on the man's head.

Guards on the other trailers were rocked by the blast and were just regaining their footing when Jerry pulled himself on top of the trailer. One of the guards spotted Jerry and shouted to the others.

The nomad gave them no chance to respond. Spraying a full magazine from the MP5, he dashed to the front of the trailer and dropped down. He fell ten feet and landed boots first on the turret gunner.

The blow made the gunner woozy; the smash of the submachine gun made him unconscious.

Jerry grabbed the man by the tactical vest and pulled him from the turret. He threw him onto the mesh grate that served as the battle platform's floor.

He dropped into the turret and examined the device. Two foot pedals controlled the rotation left and right. Everything else was aiming and triggers. Jerry mashed the left pedal and swiveled the barrel of the .50 caliber machine to bear on the truck.

Casings dropped from the weapon and piled in the turret as lead plowed into the armor plating of the rig's cab. The truck began to swerve in violent thrusts. Jerry pinned the triggers and swept the gun left and right and back again, shredding the door, the gas tank, and the wheel.

Once the rubber was gone, the rig drooped on its right side like a stroke victim. Moments later it was all over. The large plow that served as the barricade and battering ram dropped into the road and dragged the entire rig to the right.

The trailers jackknifed. The plow prevented a complete fold, but the walls of the trailers buckled and twisted. The people and equipment inside each trailer crashed about as they began to twist and bounce along the road. The trailers rolled off of their wheels.

The soldiers on top of the trailers were thrown clear. Not one of them landed well.

Jerry quickly buckled the turret harness and ducked, trusting the solid form of the plow would protect him from being entangled in the coming twisted wreckage of metal and men.

The rig shot off the side of the road and careened down a steep embankment. It dragged tons of asphalt with it down the side of the hill. Fuel gushed from the tanks and coated the ground with diesel.

Jerry's view of the world shifted as the rig threatened to roll over. Only the span of the plow kept it balanced. The truck finally came to a stop after uprooting several trees.

The trailers had not fared so well. Each had separated and rolled several times, destroying themselves as they went. Equipment and dying men littered the highway and embankment.

Jerry needed only a moment to orient himself. He unbuckled the harness and stood up from the turret.

The wreckage was still—quiet. The smell of diesel grew around

him. There was no movement from the cab. No screaming. No
pounding. No pleading for help.

Jerry stepped from the wreckage and made his way back up the
hill.

The pickup had followed the rig to the shoulder and stopped. Its
hood was still engulfed in flames from the machine gun fire. Carl
and Sheriff Deatherage beat at the flames with two old blankets that
had doubled as post-apocalyptic seat covers on the pickup's bench.

Jerry rushed to help. He grabbed the blanket from Carl and told
the short, round man to look for a fire extinguisher.

An oil leak fueled the flames. The residue spread to his blanket
and Jerry was soon waving flames at the fire. He dropped the
blanket to the highway as the fire grew on the worn cloth.

The other volunteer had more luck. He managed to smother the
flames with his blanket. Only then did he look to the wreckage of the
rig and back to Jerry. He smiled.

"Holy shit. You did it." The man panted as he spoke. Life in the
town of New Hope had never been so exciting.

"We did it," Jerry agreed and held out his hand.

"I found the extinguisher," Carl yelled from inside the cab.

The sheriff stepped forward to shake his hand. He stumbled
backwards as a bullet struck him in the shoulder. The lawman
collapsed to the ground.

Jerry looked back to the rig. The man with the white hair was
bloody and bruised, but he forced his way from the wreckage and
fired a large revolver with great accuracy.

"You son of a bitch. I'm going to kill you." The major was injured,
one foot dragged behind him as he made his way from the cab. The
stitching on his face had ripped open in the wreck. Blood poured
from the old wounds and a dozen new ones.

Carl dove into the front seat. Jerry dropped behind the pickup as
several shots bore their way past the blue and white paint. The MP5
was empty. He reached for his own .45s. Neither was there. They
must have fallen in the wreck. He pulled his knife.

The shots had stopped so he risked a peek over the hood.

The major was out of bullets. The old man stumbled and slipped as he tried to make his way up the hill. He threw away the gun and pulled the massive knife from his belt. "You're going to bleed for me, you bastard." The letter B brought blood from his lungs to his lips.

Jerry took a deep breath. It was cut short by the diesel fumes as they stung at his nose and forced him to wince.

The major was hampered with his injured leg, but Jerry also noticed that the old man struggled to find a dry surface. The oily fuel coated the side of the hill.

Jerry stepped from behind the truck.

"There you are, you coward. Get down here and finish this."

Jerry felt the heft of his knife in his right hand and the warmth of the blanket by his right leg. He looked at the major and saw not only the white-haired butcher, but every maniac the wasteland had produced. He saw the leader of the raid at Eternal Hope.

Jerry kicked the flaming blanket down the side of the hill.

It soared, trailing smoke, and landed only a few feet in front of the maniac.

The major screamed as flames erupted around him. The fire shot quickly down the fuel soaked trail. They engulfed the major. He continued to scream and charged forward swinging the wicked blade wildly at the fire.

Flames rushed toward rig's tanks and up the hill toward the 4 x 4.

"Give me the extinguisher." Jerry turned and reached into the cab. Carl tossed the red canister to the nomad. Jerry pulled the plastic ring and released the retardant at the ground. He emptied the extinguisher and stopped the fire from its ascent up the hill.

The flames at the bottom of the hill reached the tanks on the rig.

The explosion knocked Jerry back into the side of the 4 x 4.

The major was thrown to the ground.

The old man did not get up.

# 34

The explosion had echoed across the plains and reached the walls of New Hope. The column of black smoke rose as a signal in the distance. The people of the town lined the walls to watch it billow and rise until the column could no longer hold and the black soot dispersed.

They were hesitant to cheer. They didn't know that the truck had been destroyed and their town saved by the man they had discarded as a freeloader. They had grown accustomed to only assuming the worst. So the worst is what they assumed.

Erica had found an extra pair of binoculars in the motor coach and she took turns with the three boys peering through the lenses. When she handed them off, she stared blankly into the smoke and wondered if the men who had murdered her family and friends, destroyed her home, and displaced her had finally met their end at the hands of the nomad. She replayed her insults in her head as she stroked the fur of that man's dog.

All she could do was wait. She found herself hoping for his return; she hoped he wasn't maimed. Or scarred. At least, not on the face. He was a foolish man, she thought, but he was cute. She smiled at the thought of him.

. . .

Sarah turned from the smoke and looked into the courtyard. Logan was tied to the post. He dangled from his restraints and made no effort to stand. He was battered and bruised, partly at her own hand, but his eyes still shone a peaceful blue.

She walked slowly down a set of stairs and up to the restrained con man. She stopped in front of him and crossed her arms.

He tried to smile at her, but its effect was weakened by missing teeth and bleeding lips. He must have read the disgust in her eyes; he stopped smiling and looked at the ground.

"I'm sorry I let you down, Sarah."

Another kick. One more scratch. That would serve him right. She reared back to strike him again, and then she stopped. He looked as if he had suffered enough. Blood ran down his lips. His left eye was all but swollen shut. His wrists bled from the restraints, and the town had yet to get their hands on him.

"How could you?" It started soft and sad and grew to rage. "How could you? How could you?"

"I had no choice, Sarah."

"Oh, no? How about not convincing a town of innocent people to open their hearts to you while you open their gates to let them be murdered and herded into slavery? Maybe that was an option you hadn't really explored."

"They have my son, Sarah." He still wouldn't look at her.

Sarah was shocked. "Your son?"

"Yes. They've got him." Logan looked back at her. "They were going to kill him, Sarah. What could I do? What would you do?"

Sarah's mouth hung open, words were difficult. "I ..." She trailed off, trying to shake the disbelief from her mind.

"He's eight. He lost his mother when the world blew up." Logan began to weep. "He only has me. We only have each other."

Sarah rushed to him and cradled his face in her hand. She had no children, no siblings, even, but she had lost her mother. She could feel the pain of the child as the memories came rushing back.

"Please, Sarah. I have to get back to him."

She embraced him.

"If the major truly is dead, then it's over. I'm free. And I can go get him. I can get him and we can leave, together. He and I can be together again."

Sarah began to sob as well. "I can't. You know I can't."

"This life is over for me. I can start clean. Maybe I can even make amends."

She hit him in the chest; the strike wasn't hard. Her rage was gone. "You can't do this to me, you bastard."

"Sarah, please. Help me to be with my son. He's only eight and he needs me. He needs a father."

"No. I won't let you go."

"Don't punish him for my sins, for the love of God." Tears streamed from his eyes. "I have to live with what I've done. That is more punishment than any man deserves. But please, don't let my son suffer."

She looked in his eyes. She could see the suffering in the penetrating blue gaze. Sarah stood and stomped away.

Chewy saw them first. Her ears perked up and she let out a single bark. It was low and loud and brought the unnoticed silence to everyone's attention. Chewy stood and began to wag her tail, which in turn shook the entire dog.

The blue and white, and now charred, pickup crept down the road toward the town; its bed was filled with cheering children. Several more rode on the hood; they screamed with excitement.

Carl honked when he saw the spectators on the wall. The horn was weak and worn from the damage, but each blast of the horn sounded long and joyous to the awaiting crowd. Carl waved from the window and flashed the one working headlight.

Cheers exploded from those along the walls as the reality dawned on them that the threat to their town had been defeated. They hollered and rushed down the fortification stairs to move the truck. It had barely revealed an opening when Erica rushed out to meet the truck.

There must have been a dozen children in the bed and she searched each of their faces for her sister.

A smile grew on her face as she identified children from Vita Nova. She smiled and kissed each face she knew while scanning the throng of toddlers and preteens for her sister, Rebecca.

The crowd surrounded the truck and Carl was forced to stop. The people greeted the children and all but pulled Carl from the driver's seat to congratulate him.

Erica's joy dissipated as she realized that neither her sister nor Jerry were in the truck. She began to push people out of the way; she stared in the eyes of every child. She tried to ask about her sister, but her questions could not be heard over the roaring crowd.

She stopped and stood. The truck rolled past her into the town with the praise chorus following at its side.

Erica felt a warm muzzle on her hand and absentmindedly stroked Chewy's head.

Chewy barked again and darted off, forgetting all about the attention she had been getting.

"Chewy!" Erica shouted after her and made a grab for the dog's collar. Chewy didn't stop.

Erica watched the dog run off and disappear behind a cluster of trees. It was only a moment later that the dog began to walk back.

The mighty mastiff was at the heel of the post-apocalyptic nomadic warrior. Behind him was a mass of almost one hundred people. In his arms was Rebecca.

# 35

Erica squealed and began to cry as she grabbed the young child from Jerry's arms. She held her so tight that the seven-year-old began to squirm.

"You're crushing me, Erica."

Erica eased up, but only a little. "Did they hurt you?"

"No. Mrs. Thompson kept me safe."

Erica began to look at the other faces in the crowd. They smiled when they saw her. The captives from Vita Nova grabbed onto Erica. They all assumed that anyone not on the trailer with them had been killed. They flooded her with questions about loved ones left behind.

Smiles turned to tears as Erica was forced to give up the hope that had been restored by her presence. She hugged whom she could as each relived the massacre of their home. She did what she could to offer comfort, but she soon felt overwhelmed. Panic welled up in her as she looked around frantically for Jerry. She held Rebecca close and found comfort only in her hugs.

Through the crowd of people she saw Jerry walking to his motor coach. Chewy was at his heel. He opened the door and stepped inside.

Panic took hold of her. He was leaving. She fought her way

through the crowd of friends and rushed to the coach, running as
fast as Rebecca's weight would safely allow.

She got to the coach and pounded on the door. "Get out here,
now!"

Jerry opened the door.

"You can't do this now."

"But—"

"No, you can't do this and you can't give me some crap about it
being what a post-apocalyptic nomadic warrior does."

"There's—"

"No. No. You can't just ride off into the sunset."

Jerry stepped from the coach, grabbed her by the waist, covered
Rebecca's eyes, and kissed her.

Erica did not resist, her panic abating in his embrace. She kissed
him back. A moment turned into a minute. When he finally stopped
she was quiet, calm, and in love—fully in love.

"Erica, I'm not going anywhere. I'm just really, really tired and I
was going to take a nap."

"Oh. Well, if you're staying around, maybe you should kiss me
again."

Jerry smiled and obliged.

"Ewwww." Rebecca still found men, with the marked exception
of princes, gross.

Erica and Jerry chuckled at the child's response.

There was a scream.


Sarah had screamed. The scream was part fear and part frustration
that the knife at her throat was the one she had used to cut Logan's
bindings.

The warrior breathed heavily in her ear, telling her to shut up,
and threatening to cut her throat. Convincing the girl to let him go
had been easy. She had been less willing to be a hostage. He drove
the point of the blade into her flesh to make his point.

Jerry ran toward the struggling pair.

"Forget it, Bookworm." Logan positioned the girl directly

between him and the town's newest hero. "I'm leaving and Shelly is coming with me."

"It's Sarah, you bastard."

"It doesn't really matter, does it honey?"

Jerry slowed and raised his hands. "It's over, Logan. Your friends are dead. There's nowhere for you to go."

"I'll make new friends."

"You let my daughter go, you lying shit!" the mayor roared from the crowd. He had been welcoming the new residents personally. There was an election coming and a hundred new votes could really help.

"Not happening, Mayor."

"If you ..."

"This is kind of your fault, Mayor." Logan started to move toward the Mustang. "If you weren't so stupid, I wouldn't even be here."

The mayor began to protest, but Jerry signaled for him to be quiet.

"Fine. Let the girl go," Jerry gestured to the Mustang, "and you can leave."

The former prisoners began to protest. Jerry turned to them. "Listen, everybody. Shut up." He turned back to Logan, who had inched closer to his Mustang.

"Let the girl go and you can just drive away."

Logan opened the door of the Mustang and pushed Sarah's head down into the car. "No." He pushed her across the seat and sat down behind the wheel.

Sarah tried to scramble out the passenger door, but Logan grabbed a lock of her hair and pulled her back into the car.

The Mustang roared to life. The exhaust stirred dirt into the air. The spinning wheels spat gravel into the crowd. The crowd scattered, seeking cover from the tiny missiles.

Jerry broke into a sprint to the motor coach.

The Mustang sped out of town.

"Get after him! Everyone!" The mayor ran after the Ford.

"Where are you going?" Erica yelled as Jerry rushed by her.

"I've got to save her." He dashed up the steps to the coach. The door rattled shut behind him.

"But you can't catch him in this," Erica ran to the massive vehicle and tore open the door. She rushed into the cockpit. Jerry wasn't there. Chewy lay in the passenger seat, annoyed; Erica had woken her.

"Where is he?"

The dog looked puzzled and lay back down.

The rear of the coach began to rumble. The weakened walls rattled.

Erica spun and saw a panel in the rear of the cabin hanging open. It was dark beyond the small door for just a moment. Then it was flooded with sunlight.

The loading ramp crashed to the ground and Jerry jammed the transmission into first. The old Dodge charged to life down the ramp.

The crowd had begun to emerge from behind doorways and buildings. They dove for cover again as the Viper sent up another barrage of rocks. The metal walls of the town hall barn banged like thunder as the larger rocks left dents in the building. The braver ones in the group watched as the black sports car tore through town square and out into the wasteland.

Erica rushed through the garage and down the ramp of the Silver Lining. She watched the Viper disappear through the gates of the town and began to chase after it.

Logan's dog, gray and grizzled, cut her off before she could step onto the dirt of the courtyard. He bristled, his hackles raised; the mutt drooled as he growled. Teeth were missing. Those left formed a jagged smile that snapped in the air as Erica began to back away.

Three steps would take her to the safety of the motor coach's cabin. Two took her to Chewy.

She bumped into the mighty mastiff and stopped.

Chewy yawned and stepped around her to face the wasteland mongrel.

It's true that it is not the size of the dog in the fight that matters, but the size of the fight in the dog. Sometimes, however, it is simply the size of the dog.

Chewy strolled up to Logan's dog and raised her paw.

The mutt growled and stared up at the raised limb.

Chewy brought the paw down on the dog's neck and forced it to the ground. It struggled for a moment, trying to throw off the weight of the larger breed, but soon rolled over and began to whine.

Chewy let the dog stand, and offered a single mighty bark that drove the gray mutt scampering across the courtyard. The massive dog strolled back to the passenger seat to resume her nap.

Logan's dog whined as it ran into the arms of Austin the boy bear.

"A dog!"

# 36

"What are you going to do to me?"

Logan had dropped the kitchen knife in favor of a gun he had hidden in the Mustang. He held it on her as he accelerated down the open road.

"Sell you. I'm going to need something to get me started again."

"Sell me? What would your son say?"

Logan smiled and chuckled. "Son?"

Sarah stared out the window as the road flew by. Her thoughts of leaping from the car decreased as it sped up.

"I knew I shouldn't have trusted you."

"I told you not to trust me."

She sighed. "So, the whole attack?"

"Mike Jackson and Jeff Williams. Good friends of mine. Mike probably died in the truck. You killed Jeff."

"It was all staged?"

Logan shrugged. "There's usually one skeptic in town. If it's someone important, I need to do something to get them to trust me. You're the first murderer though. You should be proud."

"You're a dick."

"We do what we have to. Now, shut up. I'm trying to drive."

"My father won't let you get away with this."

"There's little he can do. There's nothing in that town that can catch this car."

Sarah's heart sank. He was right. The town had a total of three running vehicles. The battered pickup was the only one that was reliable.

She returned to staring out the window. That's when she saw the Viper in the rearview mirror. She gasped and turned to look out the rear window.

Logan saw her reaction in the corner of his eye and checked his own mirror to see what had grabbed her attention.

For a brief moment he saw Jerry in the black V-10. Then the mirror exploded into fractured shards of glass.

"Where the hell did he get that?" Logan pressed the accelerator harder and began looking for a way off the long, straight road.

Gunshots continued to pock the body of the Mustang. The bookworm was good. The holes in the rear window were confined to Logan's side of the car. Not one endangered Sarah.

Apart from weaving behind the abandoned hulks on the road, there was no place to take shelter or lose the Viper. Logan knew it was a faster car and had to do something to lose him.

He turned to fire out the rear window.

Sarah grabbed his wrist and sank her teeth into his forearm.

Logan screamed and dropped the gun in the back. It fell to the floorboard and bounced under his seat. He pulled his arm free of her grasp and smashed her across the face.

Sarah yelped as she flew into the passenger door. She sat up and spit blood at the con man. Neither was sure if it was blood from her mouth or from Logan's arm.

He struck her again, harder.

Sarah slumped over in the passenger seat, unconscious.

Logan checked the mirror. Jerry had gained tremendous ground and was bearing down on the Mustang.

Free from keeping an eye on the girl, Logan was able to put both hands on the wheel and give the post-apocalyptic nomadic warrior a run for his money.

. . .

Jerry glanced at the speedometer. It read eighty and the massive V-10 registered at a little above 1500 rpms. The open-topped car had always been a marvel to him and if he was thankful for the apocalypse in any way, it was that he was finally able to pick one up.

He had caught up to the Mustang easily and fired the warning shots to unnerve Logan. He couldn't risk killing the driver for Sarah's sake. It had seemed to work at first, as the driving had become shaky and erratic. But something had changed.

Without warning, the car had stopped swerving erratically and accelerated. Now it dodged and blocked Jerry's approaches.

Something had changed in the car. Logan was in complete control. Jerry hoped that Sarah wasn't dead.


Logan wrestled with the wheel. He cut left and right to stop Jerry from getting near the corner of his bumper. The bookworm stopped shooting. Probably from a fear of hitting the girl.

Logan smiled. Jerry's weakness had always been other people. He was too caring, too unwilling to let anyone get hurt. Pinning the disaster in Colorado on the former librarian had been easy. Jerry's guilt prevented him from questioning the situation. He simply accepted that it must have been his fault.

But the man in the car behind him wasn't the same one he had framed. It wasn't even the same man he had shamed at the gates of New Hope. This man was dangerous.

The Viper was close. He could hear the sound of Jerry's engine over his own.

Logan shoved the cigarette lighter into the dash and risked reaching into the back seat. An open crate produced several sticks of dynamite.

The lighter clicked. Logan pulled it from the dash and held it in his lips. He touched a fuse to the lighter and waited for it to burn down.

There was an off ramp approaching and Logan knew he had one chance.

Logan veered right, half expecting Jerry to lock up the brakes of the Dodge. Jerry had confided in Logan the horrors of his survival in the city. He told him about the creature that had beat upon the shelter door begging for help. How that same creature had tried, and almost succeeded, in killing Jerry and his bitch companion once the door had opened.

Jerry had shivered when telling Logan all this. His fear manifesting itself physically like that had convinced Logan of two things: Jerry would never follow him into Dallas, because whatever lived in the city terrified him.

As Logan replayed Jerry's stories in his head, he began to spook himself.

Logan hit the nitrous and increased the distance between the two cars. He threw the dynamite out the window and swerved onto the off-ramp.

The blast struck far behind the Viper.

Jerry was right behind him on the off-ramp.

"Shit."

He would have to lose Jerry in the streets.

He lit another fuse.


Jerry stayed on the Mustang's rear bumper to the end of the ramp and tapped the Ford's rear as Logan turned to the right.

The Mustang's tires smoked but found traction and sent the Ford accelerating again.

Jerry mashed the gas and caught up quickly.

Every corner gave Logan more distance.

Sticks of dynamite came quicker as the warrior behind the wheel became more desperate. This increase in frequency also led to longer fuses.

The sticks exploded harmlessly behind the Viper and posed little threat. Still, the sound of the explosions in the canopied canyon of skyscrapers pounded on his ears and shook his concentration.

Both cars weaved around the vegetation and drifted around corners as each tried to get the upper hand in the duel.

Logan had spent little time in the city. Jerry knew the streets of the town from his time living in Dallas, but, as his earlier trip through the city confirmed, the vegetation changed everything.

Any road could be a dead end. Logan feared that fact. Jerry savored it. He had no doubt that Logan would make good on his promise to make new friends. Letting him live would only allow him to dupe more people to their deaths.

He had changed allegiances before. Jerry doubted that the monsters in the truck were the same group from Colorado.

Only Logan's death would ensure that people were safe from him.

He was right on the Mustang's rear when Logan cut left, revealing a rusted SUV in Jerry's path.

Jerry swerved right and missed the wreckage but found himself heading down the wrong street.

Doubling back cost him some time, and when he got back on the street Logan had grown his lead.

A blast rocked the Viper. The stick had been close when it exploded. Jerry felt the car skid to the side, but the wide tires quickly gripped the road and put him back in control.

The cars raced down Main Street. Vines stretched from window frames and building tops and choked out the sunlight. The transition from light to shadow put his eyes in a constant state of adjustment.

As Jerry raced down the street, he noticed movement in the windows. At first, he thought it might be a trick of the light. But fear told him the truth. The creatures that spawned from his nemesis were watching.

After the day's earlier events, he had no idea what they would do.


A wall of vines grew across Houston Street, closing Main to through traffic. Logan reached the dead end that he had feared. The empty box of dynamite also presented a problem. He slammed on the brakes and slid sideways to a stop next to the wall of vegetation. Jerry raced at him in the Viper. He couldn't go back.

Light shone through breaks in the vines. He could slip through. Daylight awaited him mere feet away.

Sarah groaned as she came to. The setting confused her. "Where ..."

Logan grabbed her by the neck and pulled her from the Mustang. He snatched the gun from the back seat and shoved her through the breaks in the vines, then followed her through.

The other side of the walls of vines wasn't completely devoid of vegetation, but the wall seemed to be a barrier to the thickest growth of the jungle. The road was clear. The sky above was open.

Logan forced Sarah to run. She struggled, her head still clearing from the fog of unconsciousness. She cursed at him with every step and kept her eyes open for any opportunity to escape.


Jerry arrived moments later. He slid to a stop and jumped from the car. He burst through the wall of vines into the sunlit street.

Logan opened fire before Jerry had even gained his feet.

Jerry dropped into a roll, trying to make himself a harder target. It didn't help; a bullet struck him in the leg.

He stopped rolling and expected to be hit again. No shot was fired.

He looked up and saw Logan yelling at his empty weapon. Jerry grasped his own pistol as he struggled to his feet. The wound hurt; it burned like a torch against his skin. Despite the fire in his leg, it still supported his weight.

He limped toward Logan, who had spotted the gun in Jerry's hand. Jerry raised the weapon.

"Now wait a minute, Jerry." Logan dragged Sarah with him as he backed away from his enemy. He threw the empty gun on the ground. "Look, I'm unarmed. And you're a post-apocalyptic nomadic warrior. You can't shoot an unarmed man."

"You're thinking about cowboys." Jerry limped closer. "Cowboys can't shoot an unarmed man."

Logan grabbed Sarah in a headlock and put his hand across her face. "Come any closer and I snap her neck."

"Let her go, Logan."

Logan held the girl as a shield. His face was barely exposed behind her. He continued to drag her backward as her heels flailed to find footing.

"I'll do it, Jerry."

The bullet entered just below his right eye and blew out the upper back half of his skull. Logan fell straight back and began to bleed all over Houston Street.

Sarah was shaken, but managed to avoid going into shock.

Jerry stepped up to the body of the former con man, the gun still aimed at the bleeding corpse. Logan was splayed across a giant white X in the middle of the street. Jerry lowered the gun.

"What ... what does that X mean?" Sarah could not pull herself away from the sight of her former lover.

Jerry looked around Dealey Plaza. He looked at the vines covering the city and back at the man who had led so many to their death.

The world had changed when it came to an end. There was a lot more than fear to be afraid of. Life was worth celebrating. Death wasn't.

"It doesn't mean anything. Not anymore."

# 37

He put his arm around Sarah. "Let's get you back to town."

They walked back to the wall of vines and found a way through. He helped her into the Viper and got behind the wheel.

His leg was tender, but not immovable. Working the clutch was going to be painful, but he was confident that he could make it back to New Hope.

He turned the engine over and moved back up Main.

"Thank you." Sarah stared up at the buildings as they passed. "Thank you for saving me."

Jerry was quiet. The pain in his leg was worse than he first thought.

"Why did you do it? Why did you come back to the town? Why stop the truck? You don't owe us anything."

"Well, I—" Jerry slammed on the brakes. The Viper screeched to a stop, the wide tires grabbing the pavement.

They had moved out in front of the car and blocked the street. There were hundreds of them. The featureless plants stood in the middle of the road and swayed as if blown by the wind.

He jammed the car in reverse and looked over his shoulder. They were there, too. Quietly, they had surrounded the couple.

The silence suddenly broke. The creatures began to shriek. The horrible chorus sounded like a thousand people blowing on reeds of grass. The volume grew as more creatures filed in behind those that blocked the road.

Jerry looked around for a path. He looked for an alley, a parking garage, a lobby window to crash through. Anything. But there was no escape. There was no way out.

Unlike the Silver Lining, the Viper was stock. There were no defenses: no flames, no guns, nothing.

The creatures began to advance slowly, never really stepping forward, but leapfrogging one another. The wall of plant life came closer and closer with every shriek.

Their wailing reached a fevered pitch, the tone changing only slightly. He couldn't tell if they were getting closer, or if it was in the way they swayed, but their horrendous voices seemed to develop a rhythm. A beat formed. The pattern grew more dominant and he thought he recognized the rhythm.

The advance stopped. The creatures' shrieks changed. It seemed to go from frenzy to panic. Still, the beat continued.

He saw it first in the group in front of him. The creatures began to scatter—a few at first, followed by hundreds. They moved in waves from the back of the group to those closest to the car.

The beat grew louder, the rhythm evident, and Jerry began to sing along to the chorus of *Ring of Fire.*

The blue, white, and charred pickup rolled slowly through the fleeing throng of monsters. Erica and the three boys rode in the bed. Carl sat behind the wheel. The mayor rode shotgun, holding a loudspeaker out the window. Johnny Cash sang to the simple-minded creatures.

By the time the pickup reached the couple in the Viper, the horde was gone, their shrieking faded into the windows of the office buildings.

Sarah shot from her seat and ran to embrace her father.

Jerry stood from his seat and limped toward the truck. Erica rushed to him and held him tight.

"How many women do you intend to save in a week?"

"I think I'm done for a while." He pointed to the wound.

She put his arm over her shoulder and helped support his weight. "It looks like I get to save you now."

Jerry smiled and pointed to the truck. She helped him to it.

"Hey, Carl." Jerry rapped on the hood of the car.

"Boy, you fellas weren't easy to keep up with. If it wasn't for those pillars of smoke we may never have caught you."

"I'm glad you did. I owe you one."

"Seeing how you saved my town and everyone I hold dear, we'll call it even."

"Still, I have a favor to ask you."

"Anything."

Jerry held up the keys to the Viper. "Can you drive a stick?"

"That's what she said." Carl laughed and slapped Jerry on the shoulder.

"Don't do that, Carl. Never again, understand?"

Carl nodded.

Jerry pointed to the car. "Can you drive her back for me?"

Carl didn't say a word. He simply smiled and snagged the keys from Jerry's hand. He was almost in the driver's seat when Jerry added, "I'm going to want it back, but there's a Mustang at the end of Main you can have."

The mayor helped Erica put Jerry in the truck's passenger seat.

The three boys trampled each other trying to ride shotgun in the Dodge. Austin won and jumped over the door into the seat. He looked odd sitting there in his bear costume, but Jerry could almost see him smile through the mask.

Erica moved into the seat beside Jerry. The mayor took the wheel and they rolled out of the city, blasting Johnny Cash music the entire way.

At the Dallas city limits, Alex had them stop at the city's welcome sign. He pulled a can of spray paint from the truck and added to the green and white sign so it read, "Welcome to Dallas, must have Cash."

Jerry pondered the new sign and laughed. "I guess some things don't change."

They caught the road heading east as the sun began to set. Jerry watched it in the mirror as it touched the horizon and began a quick descent.

"Hmm."

Erica heard his mild musing and asked what he was thinking about.

"The sunset is behind me. And I'm okay with that."

**- THE END -**

**Read the rest now…**
**The Duck & Cover adventures continue in**
Knights of the Apocalypse (A Duck & Cover Adventure Book 2)

**Check out the whole Duck & Cover Adventures series here:**
Post-Apocalyptic Nomadic Warriors
Knights of the Apocalypse
Pursuit of the Apocalypse
Revenge of the Apocalypse

**And, the short stories collection**

Tales of the Apocalypse Volume 1: A Duck & Cover Collection

If you enjoyed the Duck & Cover books,
check out a different kind of apocalypse
in
JUNKERS

They stand between us and destruction.
And that's a stupid place to stand.

## Also by Benjamin Wallace

**JUNKERS**

Junkers

Junkers Season Two

**THE BULLETPROOF ADVENTURES**

**OF DAMIAN STOCKWELL**

Horror in Honduras

Terrors of Tesla

The Mechanical Menace

**DADS VS**

Dads Vs The World

Dads Vs Zombies

**OTHER BOOKS**

Tortugas Rising

**SHORT STORIES**

Commando Pandas & Other Odd Thoughts

**UNCIVIL**

UnCivil: The Immortal Engine

UnCivil: Vanderbilt's Behemoth

## About the Author

Benjamin Wallace lives in Texas where he complains about the heat.

You can email him at: contact@benjaminwallacebooks.com
To learn about the latest releases and giveaways, join his Readers'
Group.

Visit
**http://benjaminwallacebooks.com/join-my-readers-group/**
to join and get your free book now.

If you enjoyed *POST-APOCALYPTIC NOMADIC WARRIORS* please
consider leaving a review. It would be very much appreciated and
help more than you could know.

Thanks for reading, visiting, following and sharing.
-ben

**Find me online here:**
BenjaminWallaceBooks.com

facebook.com/benjaminwallaceauthor
twitter.com/BenMWallace
instagram.com/benmwallace

Made in United States
North Haven, CT
21 February 2024

49014804R00134